2022

THE DUKE'S SECOND CHANCE

CHANCE

Clean Regency Romance

JEN GEIGLE JOHNSON

FOLLOW JEN

The next book in the Lords for the Sisters of Sussex.
The Earl's Winning Wager

Jen's other published books

The Nobleman's Daughter
Two lovers in disguise

Scarlet
The Pimpernel retold

A Lady's Maid
Can she love again?

Spun of Gold
Rumplestilskin Retold

Dating the Duke
Time Travel: Regency man in NYC

Charmed by His Lordship
The antics of a fake friendship

Tabitha's Folly
Four over protective Brothers

To read Damen's Secret
The Villain's Romance

Follow her Newsletter

❦ 1 ❧

PROLOGUE CHAPTER 1

For some, the whole of their life experience is only understood with a peek into their great sorrow. Mourning never ceases. A part of those we have lost stays with us forever. For that reason, this first chapter is included.

The duchess's labor had started in the carriage while returning to their London townhome. Perhaps her pinched face and general malaise during the earlier parts of the day should have clued the duke in that all was not right, but she gave no complaint, and now he was left only to wish she had expressed a word or two of her condition earlier. He'd carried her himself into her room, her gowns wet through. At last on her bed, he was relieved she would be in the hands of someone more experienced than he who knew how to care for her. But as he brushed the hair from her forehead, as he gazed on his beloved's face, he couldn't bear to part, not yet, not with her in the utmost misery.

Gerald clasped his wife's hands in his own, hoping the strength of his love for her would scare away the pain.

Her face pinched, and she doubled over, large drops of sweat falling off her forehead. "Don't leave!"

"I'm here. Our illustrious midwife will have to unleash her dragon claws on me before I leave."

That brought a tiny laugh from his wife which gratified Gerald to no end. He tried to keep up a form of banter with Camilla who was clenched in the pains of childbirth, but in truth, if she wasn't gripping him so tightly, everyone in the room would see the trembling in his own limbs. She cried out. "It's getting worse. Is this supposed to happen?" Her eyes, wide with terror, made him frantic.

"Someone do something!" He had tried to find his deep barreling voice but the order came out more of a squeak than anything.

The midwife sidled up to him, "Pardon me, Your Grace. If I may?" She attempted to separate their hands, but he and Camilla resisted, gripping tighter. She continued, "She is doing wonderfully. Her body is performing just as we would expect it to. Everything is progressing as it should. Soon you will have a new baby."

Camilla rolled toward him onto her side, moaning and writhing on the bed.

"If I might?" The midwife repeated and gently tried again to pry their fingers apart, but Camilla clung to him. "No." Her no came out as a long drawn out syllable and he almost stepped back in fear. But her grip on him offered no mercy, and no movement.

"I'm here." He stated his determination to remain at her side. Though even to himself, his tone sounded less sure.

He hesitated one more moment, then Camilla screamed as though she were on a torture rack and released his hands, clutching instead the soothing cool fingers of their midwife; her cooing tones soothed Gerald as much as Camilla.

Gerald scooted further away. The door opened behind him. "Your Grace. I came as soon as I could."

Gerald turned. "Dr. Miller. Thank you for coming."

The doctor held the door open for him. "I'm presuming you were on your way out?"

Gerald nodded. "Yes, quite." Just for a moment he would step into the hallway.

His wife turned eyes to him, beautiful, shining eyes full of love. "I shall be finished shortly they tell me." Then her body clenched again and she curled into a ball. "Make it stop. Please make this stop."

"I love you, Camilla."

She waved him away, clenched in apparent agony.

The doctor shooed him out the door and before it closed firmly behind him, Gerald heard a quiet, "I love you too." Gerald leaned up against it, breathing heavily. What a daft thing to do, impregnate his wife.

What in the blazes was he thinking doing such a thing to them both? He closed his eyes, her scream audible through the thick door.

"Oh this will not do." His friend's voice lessened the strain that wound inside Gerald like a tight net.

Gerald whipped his eyes open, a welcoming smile interrupting the pain of his moment. "Cousin Morley. I've ruined her. She'll never forgive me, I'm certain, and she's in the most incredible pain."

Another scream interrupted. The door flung open and a maid ran out, carrying linens and a bucket. The door shut firmly after her.

Morley gripped his shoulder. "Come, man. This is not the place for husbands. Wives always seem just fine after it's all over."

"I don't know. She seemed determined I stay by her. I'm taking a break." He swallowed.

"No, they say that at first, but what woman wants you to see her in such a state? It's only going to get worse. You should have seen my sister's household. The whole place was in an upheaval, everyone thinking their lady was going to fire them all."

Gerald considered his friends words. "And when it was over, she was recovered?"

"Certainly. She was in the best of moods, gave them all an increase in pay." Morley put an arm across his shoulder. "Come. We don't belong anywhere near her. It's off to the study with your fine brandy."

Gerald nodded. "Indeed. That sounds like just the thing." He hesitated a moment more and then allowed the good will of his dearest friend to lead him along to a brighter manner in which to pass the time.

The farther away from her bedroom, the more the fibers of worry lessened, and Gerald told himself his wife was in the best of hands, that women gave birth all the time and that surely she would be well. He pushed away a persistent, niggling worry that something terrible was happening, pushed it as far as he could. For just as his friend said, what more could he do? She would be well soon enough and he could meet his son or daughter. Their lives would continue as before.

Morley made himself comfortable in the study as he always did. Leaning back in his favorite chair, he said, "Remember when we convinced Joe that his cow was about to give birth?"

Gerald snorted, almost losing his mouthful of brandy. "Clueless Joe believed us, with not a bull in sight on their estate."

Morley laughed and raised his cup in the air. "To Joe."

"To Joe."

They downed their cups, and Morley poured two new ones.

"Thanks for being here."

"Would I miss the best thing you've ever done?"

Gerald eyed him with suspicion. "That sounds very sentimental..."

"We hope. If your child is anything like *Her* Grace, then we're sure of you doing a service to society..."

"And if the child's like me?"

"Then we've just inflicted society with another Campbell, and I don't know how I feel about that."

"Being a Campbell yourself."

"Precisely. I know what a pox we are on the land."

Gerald downed his second cup, grateful for a reason to laugh. "Tell me cousin. Will there ever be another Campbell in your life?"

"If my mother has anything to say on the matter."

"And what say you? Surely someone has caught your eye?"

Morley looked away, his face drawn in an uncharacteristic frown. "I've found women to be nothing more than a silly, grappling means of entrapment." He coughed. "Present wives excluded."

Gerald sympathized with his friend. Finding a woman to marry should not be so difficult. He felt supremely lucky, blessed, in his marriage to Camilla. They had fallen in love straight away, both of them happy to pursue a courtship, their parents pleased, society approving, but he knew it wasn't so easy for most people.

"Come, man. I shall devote the next bit of my life to making you the happiest of men."

Morley held up his hands and shook his head. "Assistance not necessary. In fact, quite unwelcome."

"Think nothing of it. I want you just as happily situated as I am, for marriage has brought nothing but the best of feelings. Today's activities aside, naturally."

A man cleared his throat in the doorway.

The doctor, at last. Gerald rushed forward, shaking his hand. "Are you the first to congratulate me?"

Morley arrived at his side, his face pinched.

The doctor looked tired, older by ten years since he'd arrived. "Your Grace."

Alarm spiked through Gerald. "What is it? Camilla? Is she well? The baby?"

Dr. Miller shook his head. "We could have never known the baby would be sitting backward, that the duchess would bleed like she did..." Dr. Miller rubbed his head with a shaking hand. "I'm sorry, Your Grace."

Gerald grasped the man by the shoulders, trying to clear his mind, trying to shake the brandy from his cloudy thinking. "Speak sense man."

"We lost her." The words left the doctor's mouth in a slow motion, his face falling into a sick despairing expression.

"What?" He turned from Dr. Miller and ran to his wife's bedroom, his heart willing the doctor's words to erase. Holding his breath, wishing to erase the last hour. He pushed open the door, a maid falling to the floor on the other side as he rushed to his wife's side, lifting her frame into his arms, her sickly white skin still warm to his touch. He clutched her to his chest. "Camilla."

Her arms hung limp at her side. He lifted them, holding them close to his chest. Her neck drooped, her head hanging uselessly at her shoulders. "No." He lifted her head so it was upright. "Camilla. Can you hear me?"

Someone stood at his side. And a familiar hand clasped his shoulder. "Gerald."

He shook his head.

"Gerald."

He clenched his eyes tight, blocking out the world, blocking out Camilla's lack of response, blocking out the friend at his side, even the doctor's words.

And then a cry broke the silence. A baby's cry.

Gerald's eyes fluttered open, and his heart pounded. Turning his head, he clutched Camilla tighter. A baby cried in the arms of their midwife. He could not make sense of this infant. Why was there a baby in the room making all that racket? Didn't they know that his Camilla needed help? He blinked, trying to understand what he was seeing. Morley stepped to the side of the midwife and took the child into his arms. "Looks like you have an heir."

And then everything seemed to speed up and race

past him. And he made sense of his situation. "Take him out."

"Pardon me, Your Grace?" The midwife seemed hard of hearing all of a sudden.

"Out. Now. I don't want to lay eyes on the creature who was the cause of Camilla's death."

"Oh, but surely this slip of a thing had nothing—"

Morley placed a hand on her arm, shook his head, and the woman wisely held her tongue.

Then Morley said some nonsense about the nurse-maid before it was once again blessedly quiet. He released Camilla's dear body and placed her precisely the way she liked to sleep, on her side, with one hand under her cheek. Then he pulled the blankets up to her chin and tucked her in carefully. He was surprised by the tears that fell from his eyes, wetting every-thing. His body shuddered, his breaths coming with great effort, fighting against a new tightness that filled his chest.

He stood, unsure what to do. Did he stay by Camilla? Yes. He sat back down. But what more did she require of him? She was at rest, the ultimate rest. He stood. Who took care of such things? Her burial. Someone had to let Camilla's parents know. He covered his eyes, the wetness there again surprising him.

"Gerald."

Morley stood at his side.

Gerald turned again to his oldest friend. And the man who stood a hand taller than him, pulled him into his broad chest and hugged him like a young lad. And Gerald clung to him until his body quit shaking. Then he stepped back, at last able to take in a full breath. "What is to be done?"

"I'll take care of it. We'll notify everyone who must know. We will make arrangements for her burial."

Gerald turned back to his wife. Camilla already looked so far away. Her lifeless form had nothing to do with the vibrant soul who used to inhabit it. The light that had shone through her eyes, that broadened her smile, the laugh that had started deep in her belly and bubbled overflowing into a great and joyful music...everything that made Camilla who she was, was gone. And Gerald didn't know where she went. He reached down and placed his hand on her forehead, seeking the last bit of warmth left, finding precious little, he whispered, "Goodbye, my love, my dearest Camilla."

And allowed Morley to lead him out of the room.

❧ 2 ❧

Four months later.

Gerald's house was filled with an unacceptable noise. He'd been gone long enough that he almost forgot the presence of a child in his life.

His sister and her brood, his mother, and every now and then a baby's wailing disturbed his peace. Especially in the middle of the night it would not stop. And every sound the infant made stabbed like a knife into his heart that tried to pretend Camilla was still with him. After an interminable night, the child up every hour, waking the household with wails that disturbed even from the nursery, Gerald tried to take a bite of breakfast, alone with Morley in the breakfast room. But as soon as the food touched his lips, his mother and sister entered. "He's just ill, the poor lad. He'll be right as rain soon enough, the most adorable creature I've ever laid eyes on. Surely Gerald will see that."

They lifted their eyes, and the words died on his mother's lips. "Good morning, son."

He nodded. "Mother."

His sister, Olivia, came forward and kissed his cheek. "Good to see you brother."

The attempt he made at a smile must have been less cheery than he intended for both women teared up and rushed to the side board to fill their plates. But he didn't have any energy left to ease whatever burdens they carried. He met Morley's eyes. Solidarity. What would he do without his best friend?

He'd returned to his London townhome to mark the day of Camilla's passing. He'd mandated a household vigil, once a month, they'd pay their respects. Two days he'd been in his house, two long days, leading up to the moment when he stood, alone, in front of Camilla's grave. Everyone else had gone. He knew Morley waited for him in the carriage. But Gerald lingered. For a brief moment earlier, he'd thought he smelled her fragrance, and felt the light feather touch of her fingers on his cheek, but of course he saw nothing. He wondered again where she could be. The preacher had said comforting words about never being apart, how they carried her in their hearts, how God had welcomed her home. He'd decipher his own conclusion later.

The bright sunny day was a mockery to the darkness of his mood. He couldn't summon the energy to be angry at something so undeserving as the weather so he turned and followed the shuffling of his own feet, and climbed into his carriage. "She's really gone."

Morley didn't answer for which Gerald was grateful. As he always had been, his best friend sat at his side and just his presence gave Gerald a drop of courage. A drop was perhaps a paltry amount, but to Gerald it was everything. It was the difference between curling up on his wife's grave to sleep forever with her and going home in his carriage.

Gerald cleared his throat. "So maybe we can go straight to your apartments?"

"Hoping to avoid the woeful large eyes of your sister and mother?"

"Yes. Their assistance is torturous enough. If I start to smile, one of them looks at me and shakes their head in pity, I feel like losing it all over again." He knew they meant well, and he knew he'd be lonely if he were...alone, but sometimes he needed someone to ignore the fact that his whole purpose for happiness had left him forever.

"I don't think they'd ever forgive me for taking you away right now."

"When they have the potential for doing so much to help?"

"Exactly."

"I guess that means the ducal townhome for us."

"Is my room ready?"

"Always." Gerald paused. He really couldn't sleep in his own room, not tonight, not when it was as much Camilla's room as his. But he couldn't sleep with Morley either. They weren't lads anymore. So he closed his lips against the request that begged to come out, until the moment passed and it would be ridiculous to bring up again.

They pulled in front of the townhome, and Gerald bounded down before the footman could open the door for him. If he must face all in the house, let it be done. Perhaps if he hurried, the hours would pass quickly.

After an interminable afternoon and then evening, with everyone simply going through the motions of polite interaction, Gerald said, "I do think it's time for bed, do you not agree?"

"Oh, certainly Gerald dear." His mother approached and patted his cheek when he stood. "We're here for you my son. And tomorrow I've invited friends."

"Friends? I don't feel up for a social call; surely mother..."

"This is more than a social call. We shall discuss it tomorrow. Now, don't you worry. Olivia and I have a plan to make things right." She nodded as though something had already been decided. "No one expects official mourning for a widow with a young child. Rules are relaxed in such situations."

Gerald would always be in mourning as far as he was concerned. He hadn't the energy to decipher his mother's sentiment at the moment, so he simply bent his head to receive her kiss, received the same from his sister, bowed to the room, saluted to Morley and walked the long journey to his and Camilla's room.

But the closer he got, the heavier his feet felt until he couldn't walk another step toward the room and instead turned around to walk away from it. His feet moved faster and quicker still until he was running down the entry hall, and out the held-open door. He ran down the street, and round the corner toward Whites. No, it would be crowded. People would look at him. He must go where no one knew him, where he could hide for a moment and pretend.

Lights flickered in a small pub on the right. He reached the door and stepped inside. The place was warm and cheery, and pink, and floral.

An amused looking young woman nodded. "Hello."

"This isn't a pub."

Her laugh brightened the darkest recesses of his desperate heart. "No, it's not, love."

He looked around him. Lace table coverings. "Tea room?"

She tapped her nose. "You guessed it."

Disappointment filled him. "Well, now, what are you doing open at this hour?"

"I guess I was just holding it open for you. Would you like a cup of tea?"

He opened his mouth, ready to refuse, but then closed it again. Tea would be just the thing, in this quiet place, and the woman's voice had a cheery quality to it. No pitying stares, just a sort of friendly indifference. "There is nothing I would like more at this moment."

A pleased smile lit her face. "Then I'll have it right up." She wiped hands on her apron and moved towards the rear of the store.

Gerald sat in the nearest chair. It was made of stiff wood, painted in the usual patterns of the day. He wondered if the newest debutantes donated chairs to this shop. Each one was completely unique from another and looked to his untrained eye, to have been painted by a debutante. Did they not amuse themselves by painting such things? Chairs and tables...

He breathed deeply, leaned back and closed his eyes. *Quiet.*

China clinked in gentle sounds, and he opened his eyes.

"I thought you were asleep." Her kind eyes sparkled at him.

"No, just enjoying the quiet."

The woman poured his tea. "How do you take it?"

"Today, I think just black."

"No sugar? No cream to soften the blow?"

His eyes shot to her face. Could she know what he was dealing with? And suddenly her compassion was his undoing. Instead of wanting to remain anonymous, he wanted her to understand. Without a care, he allowed the tears to well up in his eyes. "I've lost someone who was my whole world. Four months have gone by, and I don't know where I belong."

To his great astonishment, her eyes welled up just as his had, and a single tear rolled down her cheek. "That is the most beautiful thing I've heard anyone say. She was blessed to have you, to be sure." She pulled out a chair. "May I?"

He nodded.

"Would you tell me about her?"

And he found that this precise thing was what his heart most craved. As he described his beloved Camilla, pieces of his life started to move closer to their right places in his mind, and his heart began a path to mend.

When he described how they'd met at his cousin's ball and he'd asked her to dance by mistake, their laughter mingled with their tears. Who was this woman who could feel the emotions of another so poignantly? When he talked of the day they found out she was pregnant, his heart ached anew, knowing now where that day would lead.

"And is the babe as beautiful as she?" The woman meant to continue enjoying their conversation, meant to be helpful, but the question sent Gerald to a jarring return to the present—the blame, the guilt, the immense hole in his life where Camilla wasn't and this new child was. He irrationally wanted to shun the shopkeeper, to stand and leave the shop post haste.

But she waited for a response, her kind, unsuspecting eyes ready to commune more with him. She had been such a gift to his torn apart heart that he attempted to respond. "I don't know. I haven't seen him really." He looked away, unable to meet her eyes. But she was silent for so long, that he allowed his gaze to flicker up into hers.

The acceptance and the real emotion he saw, brought tears to his eyes anew. She reached for his hand.

He allowed her to take his in her own, gloveless, calloused hands. She just held it. Every now and then she'd pat the top with her other hand. Then she said, in almost a whisper. "My mama died. And now I finally understand why my papa brushed me aside for a time." The pain in her eyes tore at him. But a fiery indignation rose up, fueled by the pain. "You could never understand. Unless you also have lost the love of your heart?"

She blinked back tears and shook her head.

He pulled his hand away. "Then you don't know."

She stood. "That may be true. But your child is all you have left of Camilla." She turned from him, carrying the tea tray with her.

He assumed he was dismissed. But he lingered a few moments more, in the quiet and empty tea room. What a gift this time had been. What a remarkable woman. He pondered what she had told him, about his son. He wasn't ready, not yet. But he knew one day he would be. One day he would cling to that boy. One day he might look into his son's eyes, see Camilla's, and not flinch away in raw grief.

As he left the door and turned to look one last time into the shop, he thought he saw movement duck away in the back. Whoever she was, he would be grateful for the gift of this time.

$\overset{\mathclap{\text{❦}}}{}$ 3 $\overset{\mathclap{\text{❧}}}{}$

Amelia Dickson watched, her eyes peeking around the back corner of her father's store, until the gentleman moved out of sight. She wrapped hands around her middle and leaned back against the wall for support. "Oh. My." She breathed. His words had been so beautiful. His face—she'd never seen anything like his face. Perfect skin. She frowned. His eyes drawn in such deep sorrow. Sharp jawline, a defined nose. She always felt that a nose made a man. She had no patience for the small and weak noses. And his stature. She'd never conversed with someone who, even in grief, owned the world. And his grief was so intense. Her face pinched in pain again, thinking of it. If his loss was anything like when she lost her mother, it would be a long time before he felt like there was a purpose in the world for him. Her heart went out to him.

And to complicate the emotions that coursed through her at such a rapid pace, when they'd looked into each other's eyes, she'd wanted to melt on the spot. They connected. Their very souls matched. She kept her hand on the wall to steady herself as she moved. Could their souls have matched? Or was she confusing her own compassion for his grief?

She squinted her eyes, trying to remember the words of her grandmother. She'd often said. "Some souls match. When the Great Carpenter created them, He cut them from the same pattern. And if they meet, they will always feel like they belong together."

Was he Amelia's match? Her soul match might rest in the heart of a gentleman? A gentleman. And one who was suffering at the loss of his love, possibly his own soul match which obviously wasn't Amelia. Of all the hopeless places to find one's soul match. Of course, she knew matches didn't have to marry. They could make their own ways in the world. Her grandmother had told her so often enough. But even knowing they could never be together, knowing she'd possibly found one somehow made her feel more whole than she ever had. The thought filled her with a completeness that wiped out the loneliness of her current situation.

She stood away from the wall, taking off her apron. She needed to get upstairs. Her father would wonder what had kept her. He'd started this tea shop because her mother had always wanted one. They built it on the very location of his family's bakery that had sat here for many decades. He'd told her the story a thousand times. And he had made their shop really successful, right here near Grosvenor Square. But he rarely descended the stairs any more. Amelia did most of the work around the place now, she and their staff.

As her feet moved up the stairs, slowly, she relived every moment with the stranger. It was perhaps for the best she never learned his name. They could never be. No matter how she felt such a connection, she could never seek him out or hope for more. She shook her head, thinking of his loss. His grief was so tender. The way he talked of his wife sent happy gooseflesh up and down her arms. Deep inside she suspected no one would ever be so eloquent in their expression of love for herself.

She shrugged. No matter. It was almost as beautiful hearing the sentiments about someone else. And the poor babe. He would learn to accept his child, just as her father had accepted her. Hopefully he would do so before too many years went by.

"Amelia?" Her father's voice sounded weak to her ears.

"Yes, Papa. We are all closed up." She found him sitting in his favorite chair watching out the window at the street below.

"Your Mama would be proud of you."

Perhaps because of the tone of the conversation she just left, Amelia's eyes welled up. "Do you think so?"

"I know so. You are everything she hoped her daughter would be." He choked up on the last word and reached an older, wrinkled hand out to cover hers. "I should have told you every day since then."

She leaned over her father and wrapped her arms around his neck. "Thank you, Father." The sweetness of his love wrapped itself around her, and she smiled.

They sat together for a few minutes more and then her father made his way to bed. But Amelia found it nearly impossible to sleep. And suddenly, an old passion resurfaced and she went in search of her charcoals and drawing papers. Lighting two candles, she set up an easel and began her sketch. Long ago, when she had an instructor, she always drew her mother's likeness from the one image her father had of her. But tonight, her thoughts turned immediately to her visitor. She suspected that if she could somehow draw her feelings, sketch them, that she would at last understand this foreign erratic beating of her heart, the tingling in her hands where she held his, and the urge to run after him in the dark.

Bold lines scratched on the paper, seeking an outline of his face. She smudged edges, rounded sharp lines, and accentuated his nose.

Late into the night, when the sketch had finally taken on a life of its own, she stared deeply into his eyes and knew that somehow, she'd lost her heart to a stranger.

❧ 4 ❧

All night, morning, and much of the afternoon passed before Gerald had any desire to participate in the household. But he joined them for tea in the front room. His mother, sister, and Morley sat close, and his mother poured. "I've invited someone to come over."

Gerald held his cup at his lips, pausing. Something in his mother's tone warned him. "Oh?"

She sniffed. One never knew what she meant by her sniffs, but this one seemed decisive. "Yes, Lady Rochester. She's recently widowed and almost out of mourning."

Alarm cascaded through him, and he stood before he placed his tea cup down. It sloshed all down his hand.

A servant immediately came to his aid with a handkerchief.

Panic raced through him and memories of Camilla filled him. "Mother." Gerald thought his tone would be sufficient to squelch any further conversation.

"Now, don't you say anything. You need someone to run your households and manage the affairs of your heir. You and she don't even have to abide together; you don't have to talk to one another except when you must organize your lives; this estate needs a duchess."

Morley shook his head. "Your Grace, surely your words are wise, but the timing—"

"Tosh. As I've said, widows with young children must be practical in their mourning. It's commonly expected that they might remarry if they so desire. The child needs a mother. Lady Rochester will be snatched up next week. If we don't move now, she will be gone." She held up her finger. "She's the most amiable sort of woman, in your same situation, and has no emotional expectations or attachments for a love match."

And immediately her words gave him pause. *No expectations.* Gerald considered. This would not be the last conversation his mother would attempt on the subject regarding any number of women. What if the next woman would expect a real relationship with him. Never. He could not betray his dear Camilla's memory. As long as he didn't think of this Lady Rochester as his wife...he shuddered again. No. Never as his wife, but as a duchess for his estate, a caretaker for his child... An immense feeling of relief filled him. Before three breaths had left his body, he gave up on denying his mother the visit. Perhaps if he just let the woman manage his affairs, all would be well. "When is she coming?"

"On the hour."

"What is her understanding of the purpose of the visit? Does she currently have any expectations?"

"Not at all, although I would guess she suspects something, given the timing of our invitation, her recent loss and yours. She, but a few weeks from the completion of her mourning." She toyed with her ribbons. Gerald had rarely seen his mother toy with anything. His concern rose when she said, "I may have mentioned something..."

"She might be as opposed as I am wont to be."

"The staff don't think so."

"The staff? What can they know about her inclinations?"

"They say that she was not overly attached to her husband and that he has left her with substantial wealth and holdings and not a drop of sorrow."

Gerald thought that odd, but he was curious to see what kind of woman his mother was trying to finagle into his life. And the truth of the matter being that ever since his time in the tea room, he'd been feeling guilty about his aversion to his son. His own son. But he didn't know what to do about it, and the child needed someone to care for him.

"Have we—named the child yet?"

"Named the child? Your heir?" His mother's tone seeped in a disapproving bile.

"Yes, Mother. We all know to which child I'm referring. Has anyone named it?"

"Of course not—"

His sister moved to sit beside him on the settee. "We all knew that one day you would want to be the one to name him."

"I best be about that, shouldn't I? Can't have this new woman here, the nursemaids and governesses alike, not knowing what to call him."

"Just so." Morley clapped him on the back. "Have you given it any thought?"

He hated to say it, but he hadn't. "I've been distracted."

"Of course. So, how about a nice strong name like Nicholas?"

"Nicholas Morley, to be exact?"

Morley sat taller. "Yes. You can tell him to be like Uncle Nicholas."

"I can't think of another I'd rather him be like, but I do believe Father'd have a disruption of his slumber and come haunt us all if the child didn't in some way carry the old Duke's name."

"And your own."

"And my own." Gerald thought for a moment more. "Let's name him Richard Gerald Campbell, the future Duke of Granbury." His mother and sister clapped. And for a moment, the mood in the room was light, friendly. After a leisurely conversation Gerald almost enjoyed, the footman entered. "A Lady Rochester to see you."

They all stood.

Gerald watched the door in a dreadful curiosity.

A woman, small in build, short in stature, stepped into the room.

Gerald exhaled his pent up breath in relief. She looked nothing like Camilla, and there was nothing attractive about her either. She might do just fine. He stepped forward and reached for her hand. "Thank you for coming Lady Rochester. I understand that you too are in mourning. I appreciate you making this exception."

She nodded and returned his bow with a curtsy of her own. "I am, though it's been almost a year for me. I'm terribly sorry to hear of your loss."

He bowed his head. "Thank you."

His mother moved forward and kissed her cheeks.

Then his sister did as well.

Lady Rochester indicated a woman who entered the room. "And this is my Aunt Bethany Spilling."

The older woman nodded to them all as she rose from her curtsey. "A pleasure to meet you all. In our states of grief." She dabbed her eyes. "What a terrible to do."

They settled in their seats, his mother poured more tea, and Gerald watched the newcomers. But he couldn't abide their presence for long. He began counting shoes to pass the time and imagined up all the ways he could leave.

Until his mother said, "And the two of you, no need to make your way alone in the world when you could go on about it together."

Gerald nearly choked. "Mother, surely there is no need to be discussing such things in an open manner."

Lady Rochester replace her cup in its saucer. "Thank you, Your Grace, but do not be overly concerned on my account. I find such frankness refreshing. I, for one, am not seeking companionship so much as I need the distraction that managing an estate grants me. And I imagine that his grace, will not have need for companionship at all from me and might be grateful if I were to take up some of the more tedious tasks of managing things, running the house, caring for the child." She dabbed her eyes. "In those ways, I feel our needs might be well matched."

He choked back a breath that he sucked in too quickly. Who was this woman in her almost alarming frankness? His mother and she were obviously in cahoots, but what next?

"He will rather I mind my way and he his, but that I take care of things so that he doesn't have to. At least for a time." She smiled, and Gerald felt as if a halo of relief had shone down on her face.

He nodded. "You have the right of it. Precisely."

Morley frowned.

"And I imagine you are wishing in this moment to find a way to amuse yourself elsewhere."

"Quite right."

Morley coughed into his hand.

Gerald stood, and so everyone in the room followed suit. They curtseyed or bowed, depending and then Morley and Gerald left together.

As soon as the door shut behind Gerald, Morley muttered, "You can't be considering this situation seriously."

Gerald paused in the hallway. "I don't even know what I'm considering."

"You hardly know her. She could be any number of things."

"But she would take care of everything and just let me live. You heard her. She's a regular staff member."

Morley snorted. "She is absolutely not. And she will have considerable power. You've your tenants to consider as well as the members of the *ton*. Give it some time. You don't even know if you can stand to be in the same room with her." He waved his hand. "So far, not for very long."

"True." He gripped his friend on the shoulder. "You have the right of it. I don't know what's come over me, but suddenly a decision unmade seems more painful than making the wrong choice."

"Promise me you'll give it some time. Four months. Six months, before even considering this hair-brained plot of your mother's."

"But what if she's snatched up?"

"You don't think you can find another woman willing to be your duchess?" Morley raised both eyebrows in obvious mockery.

"It's not that. I don't expect you to understand, but I cannot have some doe eyed beauty hoping for things from me I just can't give." He didn't voice his fear that somehow she'd remind him of his dear Camilla or that he'd forget Camilla in the face of another new debutante sharing his life.

"And she doesn't seem to care if we don't share a life."

"You're right I don't understand but I believe you and I respect that notion. I'm just saying, as your oldest friend, you do not want to rush this. There is no hurry."

Gerald nodded. "You're right. You're right." His gaze flicked to the front door. "Perhaps I'll get some air."

"Do you want company?"

"No. I need the space. I'll ask a footman to follow."

Morley studied him for a moment more. "You're going to be fine."

Gerald nodded absentmindedly. "I suppose I shall." The lie he spoke to pacify his friend felt bitter on his lips. He'd never be fine, not ever again. The door closed behind the footman.

"Stay far back. I want to pretend you aren't there."

"Very good, Your Grace."

Gerald thought he'd be meandering to the park; even in the dark it sounded like a good direction, but his feet picked up their pace, and he soon saw himself standing outside the tea room. Again the lights were on; the woman stood at the back counter, eyeing the door as if she were looking for him.

He pushed open the door and the smile that filled her face welcomed him into the warm candlelight and the flickering friendly shadows from the fire in the grate. "Hello. Again."

"Come in. I've saved some hot tea for you."

"How did you know I was coming?"

"Oh, I didn't, but something said you just might."

"Something did?"

She nodded and stepped closer to him. For a moment he thought he might have seen the doe eyed look he got from all the debutantes when he was single, but she blinked and it disappeared so quickly he knew he must have imagined it. He pulled out a chair. "May I?"

"Of course." She gathered the items for tea onto a tray and brought it to him. "Shall I pour?"

"Yes, please, but this time, I'd like my tea how I usually take it."

Her eyes sparkled in pleasure. "Which is?"

It felt so intimate to be sharing his tea preference with another outside his household, though he knew he told many a lady in many a drawing room how he'd like his tea. And he sat in a tea room, where tea preferences were shared by the fifties every day. But something about telling this woman how he'd like his tea, felt personal. "One scoop sugar. Half cream, half tea."

She nodded, poured and stirred before handing him his cup on a saucer. This time she poured herself one as well and to his surprise, made her tea just as he had. Then she sat opposite and asked, "There's something different today?"

"I hardly know... I've named my son."

"That's wonderful!"

"Yes, Richard, Gerald Campbell. After my father, and me."

"Lovely strong name."

"For a moment, I felt happy today." Guilt rose up at the admission. "But I still miss her and cannot imagine that ending any time soon."

"Of course you do." But as she studied him, her face turned calculating. "That's not it. What else?"

He shook his head. "How could you even know?"

She shrugged. "I don't know. Am I correct?"

"I would like to ask your opinion." He felt a bit sheepish that she could read him so easily. And he felt a little ridiculous saying what he was about to say. "My mother introduced me to another lady."

She leaned back, surprised.

He held up his hand. "I know. Hear me out. She's nothing like Camilla. She's not much to look at. And I feel no connection.'"

"So, you'll tell your mother no? Not to mention, it's way too soon..."

"No, I know that sounds like the sensible solution, but I was thinking about considering bringing on another Duchess."

She sucked in a breath and then cleared the expression on her face. "Bringing on."

"Yes, like a member of the staff, or something. Someone to take care of the estate, manage my son's affairs, and live...live in a different house than I."

He watched her struggle to school her features. "I see. And then..."

"What do you mean, and then?"

"Well, marriage lasts a long time. In five years, ten, twenty..."

He waved his hand, beginning to feel annoyed that she didn't support his new idea. They'd felt a real connection, like his own personal angel or something the other night, and now she was immensely annoying. "I don't suppose it matters much, does it? Since I've lost the only thing that really matters already, the rest is just waiting out my days." There, he'd said it. "And my son deserves someone to think of him."

"It seems like you have it all figured out then?"

"I think I do."

She nodded. Then sipped her tea as though they were discussing the weather.

"That's all you have to say on the matter?"

"I'm not sure what else there is to say, Your Grace."

His gaze shot to hers. Had he told her he was the duke? The way she said it sounded almost accusatory. Well, he didn't know what he'd done to be the focus of anyone's blame. Suddenly his time in this tea shop felt more stifling than comforting. He stood to leave. She slowly rose with him. They stood, not quite close, but definitely closer than they had before. The gold specks in her eyes seemed suddenly sorrowful, the turn of her nose seemed less fairylike and the very energy that seemed to bounce her on her toes fizzled. Her hair shone in the candle light. Her long slender neck open and bare. For the first time, he wondered how old she was, from whence she came and why her shop was open so late. He'd thought her a gift, perhaps otherworldly even. But here she was, a real woman, and a disapproving one at that. The obvious censure jarred him.

He bowed, crisp, the formality of the motion brought him purpose, and a detachment that he needed. Then he turned to leave. She could disapprove all she wanted. She didn't know what he faced, didn't understand what he needed.

"Goodbye." Her small voice carried to him just as the door closed behind him.

"Goodbye." His steps back to his townhome were slow but purposeful. He'd marry. Tomorrow, next week, it didn't matter. And then leave his life in the new Duchess's hands.

5

A melia's head fell into her hands at the table in the tea room. The duke? "The blooming duke." Her mother would not approve of her language, but what else could Amelia say? His signet ring had reflected the light from the fire, and she'd not mistake that coat of arms anywhere. Then he'd said his name and it had taken all her self control to maintain a calm expression. She'd entertained the duke late at night in her little tea shop, thought she had some ridiculous soul match with the... duke? The only thing she'd been right about was the incredible impossibility that he would ever be a part of her life. The presumption to talk so familiarly with a member of the peerage made her want to cower in embarrassment. The duke! "I have to stop saying duke over and over in my mind." She sat up and stared out into the darkness. "And I should really stop talking to myself."

She stood and brought the tray back to the kitchen where she used tomorrow's bucket of water to wash up the service. Every time she thought of her conversation, she cringed until each cup and saucer had been returned to its place. And then her mind turned to the duke's ridiculous plan. Was he really going to marry again so soon? To a woman he didn't know?

From what she remembered of grief, he likely imagined he'd never be happy again. And therefore didn't care what choices he made, because he was doomed to sadness.

And there was a child involved. He must get to know the woman who would be the baby's mother before marrying her. What if the woman was mean? Difficult to live with? Prone to fits of temper? She plodded up the stairs and again, instead of going to bed, she pulled out her drawings. There was a recklessness in the duke's eyes she wanted to capture, a sort of crazed abandon. Would he go through with this unwise plan? She would know when she looked into those eyes again.

The scratch of charcoal on paper should have soothed her, but she was driven with a feverish fear of discovery and a real concern the duke was about to make a huge mistake. She pushed forward as the candles burned down, and when she was finished, she stared into the intensity of his eyes and knew. He was going to ask this stranger to marry him. Tonight, if he could.

She couldn't let him do it.

How could she possibly stop him?

She shook her head, "What has any of this to do with me?" She stood up, pacing in her room. "Amelia. You are being ridiculous." The duke's life was his own. And what influence did she have? She'd had her say when he was seeking her opinion.

She stopped. The duke sought her opinion? About something so life altering as the choice of a new wife? She sat and hugged herself. What if she was the only person he was listening to? What if she'd blown it by not coming out strongly enough against such an idea?

She ran to her closet and grabbed her cloak, tip toed down the stairs and crept out the back door. She couldn't think, she just ran. The duke's townhome sat right across from the park, just up the street from her tea shop where a whole row of other members of the peerage also owned homes. And she was heading in that direction as though she belonged, not just heading, running. Her feet picked up because she knew if she stopped, she'd turn around and head right back to her correct place and station.

But she couldn't. A part of her knew she must do something. She stopped running as soon as his home was in sight. And she caught her breath. And she fought every inclination that warned her away from this place. Ladies did not call on men alone. Tea shop workers never called on the peerage, ever. She squeezed her eyes shut. Did she dare?

Instead of hiding, she stepped up to the front door. But her hand wouldn't lift the knocker. She couldn't move. Suddenly she was frozen in place in the most awkward of locations. She sucked in a deep breath and let it out slowly. Then she raised a shaky hand to the knocker. After a half breath, a tall and stately man answered. "May I help you?" His stern expression was almost enough to send her running away, but she swallowed twice and kept him waiting so long, one eyebrow rose.

Then she said, "Excuse me. I would like an audience with his grace?" Grace came out in a squeak and she wanted to kick herself, but she stood her ground.

He said. "I'm sorry but his grace is not seeing anyone. The family is in full mourning. Might I tell him who is calling? Have you a card I could leave?" He raised his nose at that suggestion. Perhaps he knew already she was not the type to be carrying or leaving cards at the homes of the peerage.

"It is actually quite urgent. Perhaps I might leave him a ... note, or use one of your cards. I'm sorry I haven't brought any of my own..."

He opened his mouth but a voice from behind, in the entryway, stopped his obviously negative response. "What is it Palling."

The butler stepped aside and indicated Amelia with his hand. "A miss..."

"Amelia Dickson."

"Amelia Dickson to see His Grace."

A tall man with kind eyes held out his hand. "Lord Morley. Pleased to meet you. Might I ask the nature of this visit?"

"Are you...are you a friend of the duke?"

His mouth twitched in amusement, but he limited the twitch and did not smile at her expense. "I am his best."

"Oh, then perhaps I might speak with you. You see, when he and I were talking earlier..."

"Excuse me, but did you say you have seen him this evening?" He stepped forward and looked up and down the street. "Would you like to come in?"

"Oh, yes, please." She looked over her shoulder. The night air was chilly and the street empty.

Lord Morley led her a short way into the home and then stepped into a study. "Do come in. I shall leave the doorway open. Most of the servants have retired to bed, but I don't want the nature of our conversation to go any further."

She nodded. "Of course."

He indicated that she sit. "Why don't you tell me what you've come to say?"

She eyed him for a moment. What she knew was a confidence the duke had shared with her probably because he assumed there was little chance she would ever share the information with anyone else. "Where is he, exactly?"

"I was hoping you could help me to discover the answer to that question. He hasn't returned."

"Oh that could very well be good news indeed."

"It is?"

"Yes, I believe so. Or the very worst." She cleared her throat. "I think he's planning to make a bold and brash move perhaps even this evening, and I've come to speak up and tell him he mustn't."

The man's eyebrows rose up into his hairline. "And how do you know the duke?"

She felt her face heat and when his eyebrows rose even further, she shook her head and waved her hands around. "No, it's not like that at all."

"Not like what, precisely?" He leaned forward in his chair. "Why don't you tell me what it is."

"I'm merely trying to determine how much he would like you to know."

"You aren't helping the conversation leave a certain assumption."

"I know. Oh good heavens, I know." She looked away, more mortified than she had ever been. "He came to my tea shop a month past, four months on the day that Camilla died."

He just stared.

"Oh, I beg your pardon. The night Her Grace passed."

"Had you ever met him before?"

"No, and I didn't know who he was. I was working late, cleaning up the shop, and hadn't locked the door or anything yet. He stepped inside and I just brought him tea like I would any other customer. But he talked and I sat with him. And." She closed her eyes, smiling at the memory. "It was nice." She shrugged. "I wondered if I'd ever seen him again, but I saw his ring just now, and I was flummoxed that I'd been sitting all chummy with the Duke of Granbury." She fanned herself. "Not that I don't serve the peerage all day long. The shop is right here in Grosvenor Square, but for a moment, I was his friend."

The man cleared his throat, interrupting her reverie.

"Yes, well, anyway, to the point, I didn't think I'd see him again. And I was pleased to help a man in such a desperate and lonely state. But he came back tonight. This time was different. He wasn't quiet and contemplative, he was frenzied and desperate. He mentioned that his mother and sister want him to remarry, that they'd chosen a woman. I suggested it was too soon."

Lord Morley held up a finger, nodded and snorted his apparent agreement.

"But he didn't seem to agree, he thought, I think he thought that bringing on a new duchess would be a way to make his life easier." She let out her breath. "And I didn't discourage him enough. I didn't know if he was serious or not, to be honest, but after he left when I looked at my sketches, I knew...I knew, he was going to make a desperate and might I be frank, unwise, move."

"And so you came here, to dissuade him?" His mouth dropped open. "You are one incredible woman."

She felt her toes heat, so embarrassed and uncomfortable at his praise. "Well, I don't know about that, but I wasn't sure what I should do. I just knew I had to try." She looked behind her. "Is the woman...here?"

"No. She's staying at her own townhome, which isn't far."

Fear twisted in her gut. "You don't suppose..."

Lord Morley stood. "Perhaps we can dissuade him together?"

"My thoughts exactly."

She hurried to the door with Lord Morley following right after. As he took his cloak from the butler, he asked, "and what has you invested in his decisions?"

"I have no idea. I just knew it was a terrible idea."

"I see. Perhaps it isn't too terrible."

"Perhaps, but the key is, we don't know, do we? Forgive me, I'm being too bold."

"After showing up here in the middle of the night to stop a perfect stranger from proposing, a duke no less, nothing you say or do will be too bold. Feel at ease."

"Thank you." She grinned. "I think."

They hurried down the street and around the next corner. The houses were as lovely but closer together. As Amelia hurried alongside Lord Morley, she still wasn't sure how she got mixed up in all of this, but she had to admit she hadn't had this much adventure in her life since...well, ever. She found herself equal parts anxious for her duke and fighting back a giggle that here she was all caught up in the inner workings and dealings of the peerage. And the tiniest part of her admitted to just being happy to see her duke again. That part of her heart knew she had to be very careful from here on out else she errantly disclose the affection of her heart in an impossible situation, even if he was her soul match.

6

Gerald leaned back up against a tree in front of Lady Rochester's house.

Was it too late to knock on the door and propose?

Undoubtedly.

But did he care? Not much.

He must care enough, because as yet, he had not moved any closer to the door, just simply rested against this tree and stared at it. When he thought of the endless life rolling out in front of him, he was torn about wanting to hand it over to someone else, hence, the duchess. Were he to tie himself to another, that endless rolling forward of his life would also *include* another. He couldn't very well ignore her forever. Something in Amelia's eyes had given him pause, the same feeling that had irritated him to no end. He'd been ready to be reckless, and now with one expression, she'd forced him to consider his actions from a different perspective. She'd brought back Morley's same concerns. Confound the woman, who was she, to reach inside him so easily and demand more from his behavior? A slip of a shop owner? He shrugged. It didn't matter. Whoever she was, however she was born, she had a certain power over him he couldn't deny. And bless her, she'd been there for him on a dark night of his life. Did he owe her opinion some consideration?

He moaned. Then he heard footsteps and low chatter. Who was out at this hour? And did he want anyone to see him, standing in front of Lady Rochester's home in the middle of the night? No, he did not. He scooted around to the other side of the tree so he would be invisible from the street. And he listened. The voices had quieted, but the footsteps drew nearer. Then a voice, he would never be more surprised to hear until he heard the next. "Do you think he'll go through with it?" His best friend in the world.

"I think he believed he would. Could he already be inside?" Amelia from the tea shop. The despair in her voice was curious to him.

He stepped out from behind the tree, and they both jumped. Amelia yelped a little bit and then held a hand over her mouth.

A light turned on in the upstairs window.

The three of them moved down the street to a darker corner several houses away. Then Gerald turned to them, looked from one to the other. Words wouldn't form. Thoughts wouldn't form. "How?"

"I couldn't let you do it." From woman from the tea shop came out at the same time that, "She showed up at the door." Exited the mouth of his friend.

"You came to my home?" He was unaccountably pleased that she would do such a thing.

"I know it was very, ridiculously, out of place for me to do so. I don't know what came over me, to be honest. But I was suddenly unable to do anything but come. You mustn't do as you'd planned."

"Mustn't I?" He'd never liked to be told what to do. In fact, shouldn't, mustn't, and can't were three of his least favorite words. But somehow coming from this remarkably bold woman, he was rather charmed instead of affronted. "And why mustn't I?"

"I'm glad you asked; for now you've given me the opportunity to say what I should have said when you first shared your hair-brained Idea." She gasped. "Beg pardon."

The duke and Lord Morley shared a look and Gerald gestured that she continue.

"I'll just say what I feel compelled to say and then leave you be. I'm not a stranger to grief. I've not lost my other half, the person who made the sun shine in my day like you said, but, when my mother passed, I thought I'd never be happy again. So nothing I did had any consequence, for life would always feel grey and void of any love or happiness, or so I thought. I really honestly didn't think I would ever be able to feel again." She shrugged. "And when you feel like that, you think none of your decisions really matter."

The duke nodded, his jaw working with an effort to control his emotion. How could she know what he felt so readily? His heart battled a whole myriad of emotions. Did his heartbreak not merit individual uniqueness? Was it the same as everyone else's? And then amazement filled him that another human could understand and put to words his grief. He admitted the tiniest flicker of hope as he leaned forward and asked, "And did the sun shine again?"

She rested a hand on his arm. "It did. And I'm relieved I didn't make any life altering decisions based on the fact that I assumed I'd never be happy again."

He rested his hand atop hers and stared into her eyes, the woman who'd been there for him now on three important moments in his life. His angel. "I don't know why this is your lot, counseling my sorry, emotionally injured self, but I'm grateful to you for trying to help me."

She watched him for several minutes more. Then hesitantly pulled her hand away. "Will that be all?" She looked from one to the other.

"Yes, thank you." Gerald nodded, unsure what more to do in such a situation.

"Are you, are you dismissing me?" The pain that flashed through her expression was quickly hidden, then she curtseyed, "Your grace, my lord." She would have left them but Lord Morley stopped her. "Miss Amelia, is it?"

"Yes."

"Thank you."

The duke nodded. "Yes, thank you. Perhaps, Morley, you could walk her home?" He turned to Lord Morley but he and Amelia both said, "No." overly loud.

He eyed them. "You're in cahoots, are you?"

Morley grinned. "Well, I just think perhaps she's right and you should at least sleep on such a large decision. If you feel urgently pressed to propose to a woman once you wake up, well, then, we'll talk about it some more. Over breakfast."

"Right." Miss Amelia nodded. "Very sensible. I'm glad you have such a friend to advise you."

Morley stepped to her side. "And I'm glad you found Miss Amelia here at just the opportune moment."

Gerald looked from one to the other, his irritation growing. "And now you're thick as thieves." His arms crossed. Miss Amelia interacting with his world somehow ruined the magic of finding her in the tea shop in the dark of night. Now she was more a regular sort of person, a bold sort of person, but not quite the emerging fairy he had almost supposed. But instead of saying something he would regret, he admitted to agreeing with their advice. "Sometimes a man just needs to wait out the night, figure things out for himself."

"I'm sorry to intrude." Miss Amelia's downturned face softened his irritation somewhat. His emotions were all over the place and he couldn't handle one more thing to worry about. Certainly didn't want to be concerned he'd hurt the feelings of a shopkeeper. "I do apologize."

"Oh, please no. You have too much to be concerned over to worry about me." Something rustled in her pocket. "Though I did want to give you this." She held out a folded piece of paper.

He took it, opening it to a remarkable likeness of himself.

"My word, that is brilliant." Lord Morley's over-exuberant praise bothered him further.

"It's your eyes that got to me. I knew I had to come."

There was a desperate glint there he didn't recognize. "Is that what I look like to you?"

"No, just earlier, in my shop."

"And you drew me after I left?"

She nodded. "It's how I used to think through a problem. Sometimes drawing it, helps me see things I normally wouldn't. Like your eyes. I knew if I could see that look again, I'd be able to guess whether you'd try to go through with your plan."

"And you felt it important enough to try to come stop me?"

"I did." She raised her chin. Her work was done. He'd seen his own desperate situation, had his best friend at his side, and she was starting to feel the cold of night sink deeper inside. "I best be going now."

Gerald looked about them. "You can't walk back alone."

She placed hands on her hips. "Well, I can't leave you here alone either."

Suddenly Gerald didn't want to stand alone against a tree in the middle of the night. "Then we'll all go together."

He pretended not to notice the looks of victory that passed between the two of them. He wasn't yet convinced that his plan was in error, but he knew he wouldn't be disturbing anyone's household in the middle of the night to carry out a reckless idea. Perhaps Amelia was correct, perhaps he just needed some time to heal before jumping to these hasty decisions.

As they approached the front door of her shop, he said, "I'm so touched you would spend your evening trying to help me. Thank you."

"You're welcome. Good night, Your Grace, my lord." Her curtsey was as lovely and well executed as any in the ton and for a moment, he wondered at her upbringing. But he had other things to concern himself with that quickly crowded out the background of his tea shop friend.

Lord Morley shook his head. "She's a remarkable person. When I opened your front door to her knocking, she looked as terrified as she was courageous."

"I can't imagine how she worked up the courage." He patted his friend on the back. "But I'm relieved she did. I was in a lonely and desperate place standing by that tree."

"Why didn't you leave? Really Gerald."

"I felt trapped." He shrugged. He couldn't explain it any better than he could understand it. "But now I've got a feather of hope again. The tiniest reason to use sense. Hopefully it sticks until morning."

"If not, I'll be here to remind you."

"And perhaps a cup of tea might be in order."

Lord Morley's eye brow rose. "Have as many cups of tea as you'd like, though I don't know how long we can prey on that woman's patience, especially when she feels responsible to make certain her advice is carried out."

Gerald laughed. "Feels right proprietary about it, doesn't she?"

"She certainly does, but thank the heavens for it."

When they arrived home, he sent Lord Morley to bed while he moved to sit behind his desk. He had piles of correspondence and at least for the moment he was feeling capable of something productive. So he sat and began sifting through his letters.

A rather larger one from his solicitor sat at the top so Gerald opened that one first. Skimming the page, he recognized a problem that would not be solved tomorrow. "What in the blazes?" One part of his estates he'd inherited recently from a cousin in Wales, included an old castle and a cottage full of women. Apparently the women, a family of sisters had lost both their parents and were left in a will to his cousin in Wales to care for. They came with the castle, as part of their own inheritance, as tenants, but the place was too old to live in, and they insisted on the gamekeeper's cottage that sat on the crossroads to town. He'd asked his solicitor how they could be rid of the whole situation. And as he skimmed the paper, he was more and more unhappy with the reply. The ladies were well respected, visited by peerage on their way to and from Brighton. And the solicitor warned in the strongest terms to do well by them and their powerful friends.

"Of all the..."

And then as he read on, the solicitor had included a list of problems with the cottage that the women were facing. As he read, he agreed, the place needed some upkeep. "Good heavens. I've inherited an expensive problem haven't I?" He began to tire. But focusing on something so odd, something so deliciously foreign felt good for a change, and he left the letter on the top of the pile to address in the morning after he'd had some rest.

He went to bed, thinking of them and their dilemma, wishing he'd never inherited them, but grateful he had something else to puzzle over rather than his own unhappiness.

7

At breakfast, Gerald wished he'd never said a word about the shopkeeper to his mother or sister. At first they over reacted to such a large degree that he'd been alone with her in a shop at night.

"Mother, no one is going to think I compromised her, nor are they going to expect me to marry her, given her station."

His mother sniffed in disapproval. "You are likely correct, but it was very bad ton. And I raised you differently."

"Mother, it was the evening of a very dark day for me..."

She patted his hand, her eyes welling with tears. "I know I know. And to think of you in this wretched state throughout your life, lonely. Could you not just be quick about your marriage? I long to see you happy once again."

Gerald couldn't answer for he and his mother had very different expectations of a marriage with Lady Francis Rochester.

"I'm relieved you aren't thinking of pulling a Marguerite."

"A who?"

Lord Morley and he looked equally puzzled.

"A Marguerite." His mother waved her hand around. "It's just something we say, those in my generation of debutantes."

Even though Gerald tried to look as uninterested as possible, she continued.

"We had quite the todo, I'll tell you." She fanned her face. "In my day, a bakery sat in the same place as that tea shop. And in it, the handsomest baker any of us had ever seen. We would walk by just to look at him. And we bought far too many biscuits and any other such thing from him, just so we could talk to him."

Gerald wished to be anywhere but here, listening to this talk.

"But Marguerite fell in love with him while the rest of us just entertained harmless flirtation. And she was convinced to run off to the anvil. She, the daughter of a Baron, and he, the shopkeeper's son." His mother clucked. "We all lost contact with her after that and you can bet we stopped frequenting the bake shop." She tapped her fan on her knee. "It soon closed. And now we have the delightful tea which of course you know."

"Thank you mother for that very enlightening tale, but you can be assured I won't be pulling a Marguerite."

"I know, darling. But you can understand why that very shop brought back the memories."

"I suppose."

Lord Morley smiled. "She is rather charming though, this shopkeeper."

"She has a name." Gerald was unaccountably irritated that Lord Morley found Miss Amelia charming.

"Oh? And what is it?"

"She is Miss Amelia Dickson."

"Dickson?" His mother's face pinched in a thoughtful way. "Dickson. Do we know that name?"

"I can't think how we would before I stumbled across her. At any rate, we know her now, and I expect us to support that shop."

"Naturally, we already do. They've the best tea around and located quite perfectly close to the park."

Gerald nodded, but felt unsatisfied. "She and Lord Morley do not think I should be marrying as quickly as you seem to wish it."

Lord Morley didn't cower when the duchess gifted him with her signature look of disapproval. "Well, I can't think they have your best interests at heart then, do they?" She turned to give her full disapproving glare to Lord Morley. "Have you thought, my lord, how your friend will fare alone? Alone. When you marry or go off on tour or other such thing, our Gerry here will be languishing alone. Have you no thought for that?"

"I do have a thought for that. Many a thought. And I am of the opinion, Your Grace, that alone would be better than some people's company."

Her mouth twitched; Gerald knew his mother wanted to smile, laugh, but instead she looked away.

The butler joined them. "A Lady Rochester to see you."

They stood. "What in the ---" Gerald pressed his lips together as Lady Rochester stepped into the room, quite alone, and dipped into a low curtsey.

"Pardon my unexpected arrival."

"You are always welcome. There will be no need for apologies particularly since it was I who invited you to call." His mother stepped forward and linked their arms as she led her to a chair near Gerald.

"Lady Rochester." He dipped his head. "It's good to see you again."

"And you as well. I'll tell you the truth of it. I couldn't sleep. Not a wink, thinking of our mutual grief compounded my own."

Gerald wasn't certain what to think of her. He was profoundly bothered that she had arrived unexpectedly. And right at the moment when he wished to discuss her with those closest to him.

Once they'd gotten over the niceties, Lady Rochester sat forward with a conspiratorial smile. "I've heard that your tenants receive regular visits from some lofty members of the peerage."

"My tenants?" Gerald started to review the tenants on his estate.

"Yes, that lovely cottage on the way to Brighton."

His mother opened her mouth, ready to deny any such tenant.

"Ah, you speak of our cousin's bequeathal."

"The very one."

"I'm just recently becoming aware of them." He wondered how she had already received news.

"A most interesting bunch, if I hear correctly. And visited by the royal dukes, no less, and the royal ladies in waiting, by royal decree."

Gerald did not know any of these details. Suddenly his new obligation to them and their dratted castle became more of an intrigue.

"I imagine they're a drain on the finances."

Gerald opened his mouth in surprise. What woman talked of the finances?

"My departed husband never managed to be bothered much with the finances. So I handled a large portion of the dealings with our steward." She cleared her throat. "And you might not be looking for anything from me at all, but I do believe the surest way to get them off your hands would be to enlist the help of these illustrious visitors and get them all married off."

"A capital idea." Though Gerald had not given it sufficient attention, he was glad of a direction to spend his energy. "Perhaps I shall pen a letter this very afternoon."

Lady Rochester nodded. "I would recommend such a thing."

"You seem to have quite a knack for running estates and a sense of how to solve problems."

She dipped her head. "I do have experience. That I will admit to."

Gerald stood, suddenly refreshed and wishing to get to know this woman better, particularly as she seemed to have an affinity for handling matters of the estate, matters that troubled him. "Might I entertain you with a walk in our gardens?"

She joined him, obviously pleased. "I would like nothing better." She placed a hand on his arm and the two of them made their way out the door.

"Your suggestions on the ladies of this cottage are thoughtful and caring and would allow me a great deal of peace of mind concerning the whole situation. But if they've no dowries?"

"I am unsure what you pay for their upkeep already, but with women so well connected, it cannot be too difficult to marry them, dowry or no. As to their looks, I cannot attest, but if any of them is a great beauty it will be all the easier."

Interesting, the way she spoke. They continued talking, mostly of matters of the estate. He ran some ideas for the tenants by her, and in every regard, her ideas were sound and her manner pleasing.

He wanted to bring up the matter of his heir. But he found difficulty thinking or talking of him, and he had no idea how to bring up the subject with this stranger. Nor did he wish to, if he were being honest. But he had to know something about her own affinity for children.

She became quiet for a moment and then she spoke in a subdued tone. "Archibald and I were not in love. We had very few intimate encounters of any kind. But we got on well enough." Her fingers pressed into his arm, and he wondered if they should stop walking so he could support her better.

"I'm well enough with all that he left me." She stopped. "But I haven't a child to love." Her eyes widened, and she looked up into his face, "and I long for one."

⚜ 8 ⚜

melia went about her day as she always had. She prepared the tea in the morning. She steeped the different brews, especially the favorites among their guests. She baked the biscuits and the scones and purchased the sandwiches. They had a cook come two days a week to assist. But Amelia chose to make some of the items herself. Unfortunately, nothing that usually brought Amelia great satisfaction could rid her of a new, festering itch of dissatisfaction. The feeling that a part of her did not belong in this life would not go away. And it was ruining her contentment. She tried not to admit that a certain Duke's smile was equally disconcerting and disruptive.

A new group of chattering ladies of the ton stepped into her shop to the tinkling of a bell on the door. Amelia curtseyed to them and led them to a table. "What kind of tea shall I bring you this morning?"

The woman who was obviously the leader, who looked to be a year or two younger than Amelia, waved her hand. "Just tea will do."

"Would you like to try our new blend with a hint of tarragon?"

The others eyed their leader warily.

"No, we would like a tea tray, some biscuits, a sandwich, that's all. And if that's too difficult to manage, we'll go elsewhere. You know we do have tea in our own houses."

Amelia's heart clenched. She couldn't afford to be upsetting these women. And their snobbery pounded home the large gulf between she and them in class and wealth.

"Well now, tea in your houses would rob you of the charm of taking tea on Grosvenor's Square with your friends." Lord Morley stood at Amelia's side, and she wanted to throw her arms around him. As she could never do such a thing, she tried to blink back her tears of relief. Why was she letting the attitudes and snobbery of the ladies of the ton disturb her peace?

She curtseyed to Lord Morley. "Welcome. Will you be joining our other guests?"

"No, I came with news."

She searched his face and couldn't tell if it were the good or bad sort of news. "I'll be right back then." She curtseyed. Then, ignoring the curious stares from every woman at the table, she hurried to the back to gather the items for their tray. When she returned, he sat at a table apart from the ladies, reading the papers and the flyers that she offered as reading material. He stood to offer to help her but she smiled and shook her head. She hurried to the ladies. "Here you go. Would you like me to pour?"

"No. Thank you."

She nodded and then, wiping her hands down her apron, she hurried to Lord Morley.

He indicated she sit with him. "Do you have a moment?"

"I do. It's quiet in here today." She sat and then waited.

He studied her. "I don't know why I feel you need to continue to be involved in our lives, but I thought you'd want to know, deserved to know after all your effort on the duke's behalf, that his grace has decided to marry after all, and in fact proposed last night."

The breath left her in a rush. She gripped the edge of the chair where she sat and tried to remember how to breathe in.

"Are you well?"

She couldn't answer. Never in her life had she swooned, or fainted, and now would she do so in front of those ladies? In front of the duke's best friend? She fought the tightness and gasped in a painful swallow of air. Then she nodded. "I'm not certain what's wrong with me. But I will say I'm disappointed."

"I as well. But it cannot be helped. I've done my best as a best friend might, and now I will have to perhaps step in if interference is needed."

"I suppose you will. You're a good friend to him."

"And he to me." Lord Morley studied her a moment more. "I'm not sure what he was thinking, coming here, but I did want to thank you for whatever you said to him, for the calm you brought him."

She felt her face heat. "I was happy to help. Good thing I hadn't closed up shop yet for the day."

Lord Morley cleared his throat. "The duchess wanted me to deliver a message for you."

Her mouth dropped open. "The duchess knows who I am?"

"Well, certainly. If a shopkeeper shows up at the front door of the townhome to pay a visit to the duke, his mother is going to hear about it."

"That sounds very brazen of me."

"I thought it brave, not brazen, and caring. You're a woman of great heart."

"Thank you." She started to stand. "I should attend to some business here in the shop. What was the message?"

"Thank you for taking a moment." He adjusted his waistcoat. "If he should come by again..."

She returned to her seat. "Yes?"

"The duchess wishes that you and I would try to encourage him in marrying again instead of the opposite."

Amazed at the notice from one so highly elevated, Amelia scoffed. "And she thinks I have influence?"

"She knows you do."

Puzzled, deeply affected, Amelia didn't know what to say. Then she wondered, "And what is your response to her grace's request?"

He grinned. "I told her I'd take it under consideration."

Amelia laughed. Then sobered. "But I could never say such a thing to her grace."

"No, it wouldn't be advisable."

She nodded then stood. "Thank you, for delivering the package. And the news. It is good to see you again."

He dipped his head. "And to see you."

Lord Morley made his way out of the store, nodding to the ladies at the other table as he did so.

Amelia hurried her package into the back before preparing tea service trays for the new guests. She worked through the rest of her day, uncertain even what to think. Then, when all was dark, and she closed up shop, she went in search of her father.

"Come in." Her father had sat by his window most of the day. "Are you expecting any late night visitors again this evening?"

She sucked in a breath. "Do you know about that?"

"Certainly. A man should know when his daughter is entertaining the duke of Granbury."

"It's not what you think, of course. His wife just passed and he came seeking comfort I believe."

"And then a visit from the Earl of Morley?"

"Is that who he is? The Duke's best friend you mean?"

"The gentleman today. Yes. He's one of the most influential men in the house of lords of late."

She nodded. "I'm happy to hear it, for he's a good friend to the duke. He seems like a good man."

"And what have they to do with you?"

"I'd like to know the answer to that question, with them so elevated and us so highly outside their sphere."

"Well, now, perhaps it's time I told you the story of your mother."

"My mother?"

"Yes. She belonged with people like those that are visiting you."

"What!" A rush of memories of her mother invaded her mind. French lessons, how to perform a curtsey, the correct manners of address...She had always made sure Amelia was taught and educated and even that she had a basic understanding of dancing and the most common Quadrilles, country dance combinations, and steps. "How can that be?"

Her father stood. "Come."

She followed him into the back room, the room their mother used for her hobbies, her drawing, her needlepoint, and where she kept many of her things. Amelia and her father had left the room much the same, each enjoying it as a piece of the woman they missed and loved. Amelia loved to go through her nice things. She had a box of jewelry. She had trunks of old dresses, ball gowns. She knew that her mother had come from a wealthy family, she'd always assumed in trade, but she'd been told they no longer had any desire to be a part of her life when she'd married Amelia's father.

Her father led her to the closet, and pulled out a box. In it was a small likeness, a painting of a noble woman, of her mother.

"Your mother."

"She's lovely."

"At her coming out ball."

Amelia puckered her mouth in confusion. "She had a ... coming out ball?"

"She did. And she was pursued by many a gentleman. But that's when she started making visits to my father's bakery."

"And to you?"

He nodded, a twinkle lighting his face. "We stole every moment we could. So in love we were, we begged our parents to approve, but neither could condone what they thought would be a life of unhappiness for the both of us. Her family opposed most of all."

"But why? Was the bakery not a respectable establishment?"

"Oh, it was. Every member of the ton came for my father's tarts, his cakes, his breads. Even the big estate homes would make orders for their balls, dinners, parties."

"Then what was the problem?"

"Your mother was the daughter of a Baron."

"What? A member of the peerage?"

"Yes, and they knew that by lowering herself, she'd come against criticism and shunning."

"But she wanted to marry anyway?"

"She did." He sat up proudly. "We both did. So we told everyone what we were about and then we rode a carriage up to Scotland, married across the anvil."

Amelia sat back in amazement. "And her family wanted nothing more to do with us?"

"They thought they would protect us. It was better for us to be forgotten for a time, I thought, perhaps forever. The bakery failed. The family moved away. We stayed quiet for many years, letting the gossip die down. And then we thought to start up a new tea shop in our old bakery space, with no one knowing we were the same that had caused such a scandal."

"So, my grandfather is a Baron. A...lord?"

"They call him Lord Smithson."

She sat on her mother's bed. "I cannot believe it."

Her father's presence beside her made her smile.

"She raised you to be one of them. All those things you can do, the greetings, the curtseys the rules, your drawing, your language, all of it."

"But..."

Her father pulled a letter out of his pocket. "And this arrived today."

"What is it?" She noticed a seal in deep blue wax.

"It's addressed to you. From your grandfather."

She reached for the outstretched letter and weighed it in her fingers. "What does he want?"

"Well, I don't know as you've not read it yet."

"Should I read it?" Her hands trembled so she rested them and the letter in her lap.

"I'll leave that up to you. They've been writing your mother all this time. They are good people. But they didn't come when you were born, didn't come to your christening and haven't even stepped foot inside the shop. So you decide if they deserve your attention.

I've forgiven them years ago, but that's up to you to decide if you'll do the same."

She had nothing to hold against them. She'd led the happiest of lives, born to parents who doted on her, gifted a tea shop to run and one day own. She didn't think anything a Baron could offer her would have been any more enjoyable or content. But as her fingers pushed through the wax and broke the seal, she couldn't help but think again of the Duke. She had no offers of marriage in her life, no possible courtships, and no opportunities to rise above her station in any way. That familiar tickle of the last few days festered again inside.

She lifted the parchment and unfolded her letter.

It was written in an elegant hand, the letters slanting and sweeping across the page.

"My dearest Amelia Dickson,

If I might call you dearest.

I'm writing with the greatest desire for you to come to me, dine with your grandmother and I so that we might become better acquainted."

It was signed by her grandfather.

"They want me to dine with them."

"Excellent."

"But not you?"

"I don't suppose I will ever be invited to their home, on principle."

Irritation surged up inside. "Then I shan't go either."

"That's your mother in ye. She'd never go. If I wasn't welcome, then she wasn't going. But I think you might reconsider this stance."

Amelia was unaccountably proud of her mother and had no inclination to do any differently.

"Consider that they're your family too. They have their reasons. The peerage are trapped into a way of being and thinking that makes them unable to entertain me as a part of their family. The only way they saved themselves from the scandal of our elopement was by shutting us off."

"Why would I ever want to ensnare myself in such a society?"

"Because they're lovely people, who will love you. You have a whole side of the family over there, and what's more, people to care for you."

Her father seemed weak all of a sudden and Amelia recognized the throws of age wrapped themselves around him.

"When I'm no longer here, it'll bring me peace knowing that you have others who care for you."

She studied her father and she could see what a burden would be lifted if she did indeed begin a new sort of relationship with the Smithsons. So she nodded. "Then I'll go."

Her father patted her hand. "That's a good choice, Amelia." He stood, his legs shaking a bit from the effort. "And now I'll be heading my way into bed for the evening."

"Get rest father. And thank you."

"Oh, and best to answer that letter. I'll have it delivered tomorrow."

"Thank you, I will."

She pulled out a quill, ink well, and paper. Now, what to say to the family who wouldn't acknowledge her for all these years?

After puzzling for too long, she simply thanked them for the invitation, and said she would be ready for their carriage tomorrow. Done.

9

Gerald's mind turned unaccountably to Miss Amelia Dickson too many times. His fiancé would arrive any moment. And he'd not told Miss Amelia that he ignored her advice. Perhaps he felt he owed her an explanation. But the notion was ridiculous. How and when did he as a duke owe a tea shop keeper any explanation for anything?

Lady Rochester stepped into the room. "Are we to meet young Richard Gerald?"

Gerald clenched his fists behind his back. But he was determined not to be nervous, or emotional about this. If he could introduce his soon to be duchess to his heir, then the two of them could get along fittingly, and he could be on his way. "We are. The nurse will bring him down in a moment."

"Oh, I'm glad to hear it. I cannot function as his—" She stopped what she was about to say, her eyes growing wider before she corrected, "As the duchess, without knowing him properly." She wrung her hands. "You do think he will like me, don't you?"

"I don't know why not. He's but a small thing still. Might not even know how to like a person."

"But babies can tell. And if they don't like a person, most everyone else won't trust them either. Oh, my, oh dear. Perhaps we should meet him another day when I'm not so stressed?"

"If you would like, but I do think you shall be just fine. And we won't hold it against you if the infant isn't quite sure of you yet."

She patted his arm and he tried not to flinch.

"To be honest, I haven't met him yet either, not really."

The aghast expression she gave him should have been his first warning as to what kind of woman he was welcoming into his life.

"You haven't met him? The tiny child who looks to you as his father?"

He turned away. "I don't wish to discuss this with you. Perhaps you're correct. Perhaps today isn't the best day." He wanted her out of his sight sooner rather than later.

But the double doors opened, and the nurse entered, carrying his son. And all thought left his mind, everything but the profile of a beautiful boy, looking up from the nurse's arms, into her face. And all he could see was his wife's nose, Camilla's. And suddenly, seeing his wife in another, endeared him instead of repulsed him. "There now, look. He's just a small baby. Nothing to worry about in him." He reached for the baby from the nurse, whose eyes widened in pleased surprise.

As he curved his hands around the tiny infant, the boy felt smaller than he was expecting. And more wobbly.

"Support him, like this." The nurse helped to guide his hands.

Gerald adjusted the child and fumbled a bit.

"Perhaps we should sit down?" The nurse's voice was gentle, suggesting, and she pointed to a nearby settee.

"How dare you speak to his grace like that? Or sit in his presence?"

"Lady Rochester, I really don't think now's the time..."

"Every time is the time to be respectful in this house. Imagine if she's forgetting her place now, what she might do with your son when you're not around."

Gerald heard the tiny intake of breath from Joanna, the nurse they'd hand-picked months ago, who Camilla loved. "Lady Rochester you have overstepped. This woman is like a member of our family and has—"

"You're taking her side over mine?" Much to Gerald's shock, Lady Rochester put her hands over her face and commenced wailing out large sobbing sounds.

"What?"

The nurse turned to him in sympathy and offered to take the child but he eyed Lady Rochester and shook his head. Then turned his attention back to his son.

Lady Rochester's wails grew louder and a footman stepped into the room. Gerald indicated with his head that the caterwauler needed to exit the room and so the footman stepped closer to her as two more maids joined him. He bowed. "Might I escort you somewhere to freshen up. The duke has asked for a service to be placed in the lovely blue room."

"I will not be escorted from the room as though I'm a common street urchin. I'll go where I please. This will soon be my house as well as anyone's and I will be listened to." Her shouts became more sporadic and high pitched and baby Richard startled twice before his own face pinched in sadness and then Gerald witnessed the saddest and most beautiful cry he'd ever seen. His son's face turned red and he cried out in response to Lady Rochester.

Gerald handed him back to the nurse with great regret. "Could you bring him to me this evening? I think I'd like to get to know my son."

"Yes, Your Grace." She curtseyed and fled from the room.

Then Gerald approached Lady Rochester, unsure how she would react. As soon as she saw him, she reached for his arm and clung to it.

"Let's get you situated in the room my staff suggests as it has been prepared especially for you." If he could but keep her happy for a moment, keep her amenable to moving to another room, to leaving his home, then he could determine his best course of action after.

She sniffed. "Oh, it has?"

"Yes, certainly. And then we will see what we can do to ease your worry."

She patted his arm. "You are all that is goodness. Thank you. And don't you worry. We'll get your staff and your nurse all situated. They'll soon understand how they must be treating a duke and a duchess."

He just nodded to keep her from making any more noise and led her to the front room, the blue room. He was pleased that a pleasant looking tea had been set up as well as a tray of breads and cheeses. "There you are. This should suit just fine while you catch your breath, relax a moment before we try again to meet my son."

When Gerald turned to go, she shrieked, "Where are you going?"

"I thought I would answer some correspondence in my study while you reconstitute yourself."

"You'd leave me here alone?"

"Well, I thought—" He knew whatever response he gave would be fruitless. When he turned to re-enter the room, her face filled with satisfaction.

He ground his teeth and returned to his fiancé's side. His stomach grew heavier, his heart beat faster, and his head started to pound the more he realized that he had made a terrible mistake.

She chattered away about anything and everything nonsensical. He stopped listening within the first few moments. But he wasn't sure he was permitted to leave her side yet, without her making a scene. And truly, he was hoping to spare the staff. Since when had he become so concerned with the staff?

He knew when. When he'd lost Camilla. She had loved and respected them. They'd treated her well. He was grateful for them.

Palling entered the room. "Excuse me, Your Grace. There's a matter of some urgency to attend to in your study."

Gerald stood.

"You are not permitted to interrupt us."

He turned, slowly. "Excuse me?"

"The staff. They mustn't interrupt us. When we are having a moment, they are to stay away. I cannot countenance you leaving right now. How do we even know it is urgent as he says?"

Palling's expression did not change. But Gerald's did, and Lady Rochester sat back in surprise. He must have looked more fierce than he meant for she dipped her head in her hands. "And now you're displeased with me." Her soft cries were almost more painful than her wails. He looked helplessly about until he caught sight of Morley in the hallway. He bowed to her unseeing figure and hurried out of the room, Palling closing the door behind him.

Gerald rushed to his friend. "She's a storm of the

worst kind, a crazy woman. Demanding all sorts of things. I don't know that I'd have dared leave her side were it not for my summons. Was that you?"

When Lord Morley nodded, he hugged him. "Thank you. I owe you, whatever you want."

"Come, let's talk in your study."

A loud crash came from behind the door. Gerald winced, stiffened, and then shook his head. "Palling."

"I'll take care of it, Your Grace."

"I don't mind if she must leave."

"Very good, Your Grace."

Another crash and a series of incredibly loud shrieks followed. Gerald was certain the neighbors on both sides heard. He looked to Lord Morley but his friend indicated they keep walking, picked up their pace and closed the door tightly behind Gerald once he was inside.

The caterwauling grew louder outside his door, following by the soothing tones of his housekeeper. Feet from many of the household footmen answered, and then "I will have every one of your fired the day after the wedding. How dare you throw me from this home. I am not finished."

"We thank you for coming. His grace has asked that we ensure your utmost comfort while escorting you out. Would you like the carriage?"

Before she could answer, Palling answered. "It has arrived. Our finest footman will escort you out and place you inside to ensure you are taken care of in the best manner possible."

Morley and Gerald eyed each other. "Your staff really are remarkable."

"Yes. I'll be giving them a little extra this week." He ran a hand along his forehead. "What have I done?"

"Thank all that's good in this world you haven't gone and married her."

"But I'm engaged, aren't I?"

"No amount of scandal can be too much to overcome when the other option is what you've just gently thrown from your house."

Gerald shuddered. "I agree, but what's to be done? I'm afraid to break it off. What if she hurdles something at my head?"

His oldest friend just shook his head. "If you're man enough to get yourself into this mess, Your Grace, then you're of the caliber that can extricate yourself, I'm certain."

"Is that your not so delicate manner in which to remind me that if I'd listened to you I wouldn't be in this bind in the first place?"

"I am in fact parading that reminder out in front of you this moment." He moved the fingers of his hand as though they were marching.

"Oh stop. So, Lord know it all, what do I do now?"

Footsteps sounded outside his door and a swift knock followed. "Enter."

Palling stood in the entryway with a footman and a maid. She had a large scratch across her cheek.

Gerald stood. "Good heavens. What's happened?"

Palling said, "Go on now, tell his grace, you've done nothing wrong."

"No, certainly. Please feel free to be frank. You won't be punished."

"She said I'd be thrown out on my duff." She gasped. "Forgive my language."

Gerald hid a smile, but the horror inside grew. "Lady Rochester?"

"Yes, she started wailing louder the further we went, then she started swinging her hands about and grabbing at our hair. We weren't sure what to be doing, with her screaming threats and the like, but she don't live far, and we've that to be grateful for. We arrived in front of her home, she making enough noise to wake the whole street, and I did see many a faces in the windows of her neighbors, mind ye. But her door opened with what looked like half the staff coming out to meet her."

The footman nodded.

"And they consoled her in their own way, and we were told to go back, that we'd all be hearing from her."

Gerald cleared his throat. "Your name?"

"Lisbeth."

"Lisbeth, thank you for what you've done. Would you mind going down to the kitchen to see what can be done about that scrape. Please accept my deepest gratitude. And to you as well." He include the footman in his praise. "And to you Palling." Gerald shook his head.

"Our pleasure to serve you, Your Grace. I knew you'd want a report and since we have no way of knowing what she will say about her treatment from us, wanted you to hear it from us first."

"Certainly. And feel comforted that your positions are safe here in my house. Thank you."

They left and closed the door after.

Lord Morley handed him a brandy without speaking. And they stared at the wall for many minutes before someone knocked on the door again. "Enter."

The servant had the silver tray with a letter.

Gerald broke the seal, assuming it to be from Lady Rochester.

The more he read, the more difficult he found it to do anything but frown. Words failed him, movement became more difficult. When he didn't think he would breathe well for very much longer, he handed the letter to Lord Morley to read.

"From Lady Rochester's brother? The Earl of Hamden?"

Gerald nodded.

"Your grace etcetera. Etcetera.

The treatment of Lady Rochester in your home has worsened her state to such that she is no longer consolable. She is ranting and crying and carrying on. And promises that all will be well again once she's married."

Lord Morley opened his mouth to say something, but Gerald waved that he should continue.

"*As the scandal of her public episode on our street is likely spreading through the ton and the upcoming scandal of a break in your engagement would surely ruin her, I ask that as a gentleman, you preserve her reputation and put her away in a house, grant her servants and protection, and save all of us from further embarrassment. Her estate can afford such a situation.*"

Lord Morley ran a hand through his hair. "He cannot expect you to do this."

"She has the means. I wouldn't be even footing the expense, just overseeing it, I gather."

"But were people to discover, they would assume all manner of things."

"I know. And I'd be forced to continue in a charade of an engagement."

"You'd be unable to marry anyone else if that is still a goal." Lord Morley's grimace showed Gerald precisely how awful an idea he thought marrying would be.

"All things considered, I believe this is the thing to be done. For now."

"What exactly ails her?"

"He didn't say, but he did mention her state worsening, so perhaps she's a problem already, before her great upset today."

"Yes, I believe so. But she was perfectly reasonable not two days past."

"She was, at least during the few moments you spent time with her."

Gerald shook his head. "Think how many women we know could be absolutely bound for bedlam."

Lord Morley shuddered. "Makes a man confirm his bachelorhood."

"Or miss his wife." Gerald's face crumbled. He couldn't hold it together any longer. All the horrifying moments, the struggle to remarry and keep it emotionless, seeing his son for the first time, really seeing him... He stood and rang his bell.

When Palling came, he said, "Will you see if the heir is awake and agreeable to seeing me?"

The butler's mouth twitched, but only for a second, then he said, "very good, Your Grace."

He turned to Morley. "You have to see my son. He's the handsomest lad I've ever laid eyes on."

Lord Morley's grin grew. "He is indeed."

"You've seen him?" He smacked his forehead. "Oh, of course you have!" He'd been there when the child was born.

"I stop by the nursery every day. He's laughing now, you know."

Gerald stopped. "You what? He's laughing?" A part of him thrilled at the thought. "I missed it?" Fists, clenched around his heart, squeezing just enough.

"Well, now, he'll do it again, I'm certain."

The fists loosened their grip. A knock at the door made him jump to his feet, and then Palling's voice announced, "His Lordship, Lord Richard to see you, Your Grace."

Gerald laughed. "Come in, my son. Let's hear this laugh of yours."

❧ 10 ❧

Amelia put on the best dress she could find which was nowhere near as nice as any of the typical finery of the ladies of the ton. She stood in front of her mother's mirror.

"That brooch looks good on you. Reminds me of your mother."

"She was so beautiful." She lifted the image they had of her, young, happy. "I'm afraid I'll feel out of place."

"You might. But they're your family, sure as I'm standing here, and your mother loved them."

She stood taller and gathered courage from that declaration. "And they requested the meeting. So they must want to see me. Is—What kind of man is grandfather?"

"Well, now, from the way your mother would talk of him, he was funny. Had twinkling eyes, I do believe she was his favorite."

"And grandmother?"

"I think she might be the more stodgy one of the family, more bent on the rules, but in the end, she was the one who wrote your mother the most."

The sound of a carriage approaching made her suck in her breath. She straightened, clutched her mother's reticule, and tiptoed up to leave a kiss on her father's cheek.

"Just remember all the titles in the world don't mean a thing if you don't like the people who hold the titles."

"I know, Papa. I'll be back soon."

He followed her to the door, ready to take on the tea shop duties for the morning.

She exited and a footman bowed and opened the door to a lovely carriage. The outside was dark, with a sheen that reflected the sun. The horses stamped impatiently. The coachman sat on top, facing forward, the livery a deep blue. She couldn't believe she was about to step inside such a vehicle. She used the foot-man's hand to steady herself as she climbed the steps and blinked to adjust to the darker interior. The plush seats were a rich red. "Lovely."

"Thank you."

Amelia bit the inside of her cheek to keep from calling out in surprise she was not alone. She situated herself, facing the woman already seated in the carriage and then barely whispered, "You're welcome."

More bony than soft, the woman eyed her for many moments without speaking. She was stately. Held herself in one tight rod, but her eyes were kind. She had smile wrinkles which gave Amelia hope as to her nature. The carriage began moving. Amelia felt none of the jerking motions she normally associated with the start of motion in a carriage. But she couldn't relax into the gentle rocking motions of the finely equipped vehicle. She folded her hands in her lap, crossed her ankles, and waited to be spoken to, belying the intense energy coursing through her.

At length the woman shifted. "I'm pleased you could join us."

"Thank you. I am honored to be thought of." She still had no clue as to the identity of the woman. She might harbor a guess, but daren't.

"You have a great deal of your father in you." Her tone spoke neither approval nor disapproval.

"Are you acquainted with my father?"

"A very little, though he was quite looked upon by the ladies of the ton. I daresay those in my generation would all recognize him if they knew where to look."

Amelia nodded, unsure what was expected.

"But I do see your mother in you as well. There, in the set of your chin, in the dancing uncertainty behind your eyes. You're full of energy, aren't you child?"

A nervous giggle escaped and Amelia grinned. "Oh, my. Yes, I am." Amelia forced her legs to remain still and kept her hands firmly clasped.

"Your mother has taught you well."

"Please. Might I know who you are?"

"Oh, of all the ridiculous... Imagine introducing myself to my own granddaughter." She dipped her head. "I am Lady Smithson." She held her hand out. "Come here."

Amelia moved to sit on the bench beside her and felt the bony arms encircle her shoulders. "Lady Smithson?"

"Yes, but you must call me grandmother."

Amelia sucked in her breath. "Truly?"

"Yes, dear, oh yes, and I am sorry it has taken so long for us to meet. But let's not linger there. All can be discussed at great length later. For now, your grandfather and I are pleased to invite you to our home."

They pulled in front of a modest looking townhome, much grander than Amelia would ever imagine living in, but not so grand by half as that of the duke. As those are the only homes Amelia had to compare, she thought her grandparents quite pleasantly situated.

"We share a park block with the homes you see on our sides and behind. A courtyard in the middle."

"Oh lovely."

"Perhaps we shall take a turn after tea."

"Yes, I would enjoy that very much."

"Your grandfather will be pleased to hear it as he spends a great deal of time tending it, pestering the gardeners and reading there himself."

He sounded lovely. The longer she was in her grand-mother's company the more relaxed she felt.

The footman helped her down and within two steps, a giant of a man, looked to be quite a bit older than her father, came bounding down the steps and stood in front of her. "Amelia? Could this be our baby Amelia?"

Amelia laughed and curtseyed. "My lord."

"Oh tosh. Who stands by ceremony with family? Come here." He held out his arms and when she tentatively stepped into his offered embrace, he squeezed her close. But his hands were gentle, questioning and when she stepped back, his eyes, misty. "Thank you for coming."

"You're welcome."

He led them into the house which was comfortable and fine. Before she had time to think much else, they were seated, and the servants were setting out tea.

"Would you mind pouring, my dear? My hands shake so, I find it better to let the younger ladies do the honors."

"Certainly." Amelia smiled. Tea was a simple enough request. She poured and stirred, and placed biscuits and sandwiches on trays without thinking much about it.

When they each had their plates and tea just as they wished it, her grandfather leaned back in his seat. "I can't tell you how pleased I am to have you here in our home."

He nodded. They both replaced cups on their saucers. "When you grow older you realize more poignantly what you truly love. And we wish for you to be a part of our lives."

She stared back in wonder and surprise. "Truly?"

"We've wished such a thing for years. Almost as soon as your mother left."

"But haven't you been writing mother?"

"We have, and ..." She raised her hands.

Then her grandmother leaned forward, shook her head at her husband and said, "I suggest we be open. There are some things that we aren't really proud of and others that are just the reality of our lives and must be understood."

"I'd like for you to be honest with me."

"When your mother ran away to get married to someone from an entirely different class, it caused a scandal the likes of which we'd never seen."

"To protect us all, your mother included, the family ran away to the country and completely disappeared from society. Even from our lives. They thought that if they disappeared for long enough, people would forget, and it worked, we didn't even know they'd returned, or set up the tea shop for many years."

Her grandfather shook his head and patted her hand. "To think we didn't even know our grand-daughter was but a few streets over."

"But how did you finally discover me?"

"Your father."

"What?"

"Yes, he reached out and let us know, said he thought it was for the best, if we wanted to be a part of your life."

Her grandmother clasped her hands together. "Which of course we do want to be a part of your life."

"We want that more than anything else." Her grandfather rubbed his eyes. "When I think of all the years we've missed..."

"And my father?"

"Your father?"

"Why isn't he invited to come have tea?"

The pause grew more uncomfortable the longer it lasted. "He's from outside our world. He understands that."

Amelia felt a strange, awkward sort of pain divide her in two.

"We'd like to sponsor you, for a season."

"What?"

"Yes, and give you everything you should have had if your mother had married within her station."

"I-I don't know."

"Please, allow us this one thing. Allow us to make up for all the lost time."

"But what of my station, those who will recognize me, from the tea room. Won't the scandal you've all been avoiding blow up?"

"We don't think so. We've some powerful women on our side with this. Friends of your grandmother's. And of course you must stop working in the tea room."

"And your grandfather is highly respected." She leaned forward. "There are many who will welcome you out of love and respect for our family." Her eyes widened hopefully.

"Well, of course, if you put it that way."

She clapped her hands, smile growing. "I'd love to start on your wardrobe right away. Do you have time tomorrow to visit the modiste?"

What! A real modiste. This was starting to sound like one of those stories in the books her mother kept.

Even after telling her father all about the visit, she couldn't quite believe what was happening to her. "Why didn't you tell me all of this sooner?"

Her father shook his head. "Because we honestly believed there would never come a time you would need to know, that we would never feel it important to find that old way of life again. We thought it was better for all involved."

"But now?"

"Now, I'm getting weaker."

Her next words caught in her throat. She knew. She'd noticed, of course. Whatever ailed him was taking over more and more of his body.

"And why don't you come with me?"

"It wouldn't be fitting."

"I don't see how you can feel that way. Mother loved you, their own child. You are the father of their granddaughter..."

He held up his hands. "You don't understand because we haven't raised you to think in the same manner that they think, but this is for the best. It is better for you as well, if I'm not a part of your coming out, or your new life in the ton."

"Not a part of my life?"

"Of course I'm always your father." Her father's head started to droop and his eyes close.

"Go, I'll clean up."

He creaked to his feet. "Thank you daughter. I'm happy they want to be a part of your life. They'll be better off just for knowing you."

She kissed his cheek. "Good night, father. They'd be better off knowing you as well."

He waved to her as he left the kitchen and climbed the stairs as though the weight of their concerns rested in each shoe.

While Amelia wiped down tables and then swept the floor, the whole of her interaction at her grandfather's home replayed in her mind. *A season.* She'd often imagined herself wearing her mother's beautiful clothes, dancing the dances she'd taught her, curtseying before the handsome lords and whirling around the dance floor. Could this be happening?

Without her mother. Just the thought lowered the corner of her mouth. She missed her mother with an ache that found no relief. And she would miss her abominably as she heard her name announced to a ballroom full of people.

She couldn't see her mother in her grandmother. Or her grandfather. Perhaps she looked like an aunt. She'd like to see the portrait gallery next time she visited.

The door creaked open, and she remembered she hadn't locked up yet. As she rounded the back, to see who had come in, she stopped and smiled. "Hello."

Her duke stood in the middle of the floor, shifting his weight from foot to foot.

"Well, come in."

He approached. "I did it."

"Did what"

"Proposed."

"I know."

"How could you know?"

"Lord Morley stopped by to tell me."

"Did he now?" His mouth frowned for a moment but then he said, "Can we sit?"

"Yes, of course, would you like some tea?"

"Not tonight. You've already washed up."

So she joined him. Sat at a table with him, no tea, not a biscuit in sight. And it felt odd, and strangely liberating at the same time.

When he didn't say anything for the first few moments, she asked, "Are you happy?"

Then he snorted. And held his head in his hands. "Oh, I've made the biggest muck of things, and neither Lord Morley nor I have any idea what to do about it." He looked up. "That is, we have an idea, but I've put myself in the biggest bind, even bigger than the one I thought I was entrapping myself in."

"This sounds ominous. Surely it isn't as terrible as you say."

"Worse. For not only am I well and truly engaged to Lady Rochester, but she's also well and truly losing her mind."

"What?" Surely he jested. But his expression remained deadly serious.

And she waited while he explained the whole of his dealings with Lady Rochester.

"We are travelling down towards Brighton, for we've a home there she could stay in, with her own staff, to keep herself safe and, honestly, far from us. Her brother thought it the best idea."

"And you're to stay engaged?" She felt most distraught about that piece of news. Though she had no right to be.

"Yes. I'm well and truly flummoxed. What shall I do?"

"I don't see how you can escape the engagement without scandal. But..."

"Yes?" He leaned forward, clearly hanging on her every word.

"But does it matter?"

"Matter?"

"Right. Is not your happiness worth more to you than your reputation?"

He sat back and looked at her as though she spoke another language entirely. "Worth more than my reputation? Of course not."

She nodded and tilted her head, trying to understand. "Then I guess you will stay affianced until your happiness is contested, and you must make a different choice to retrieve it."

He adjusted his hand so that it rested on the table close to hers. Then he leaned forward so that he could look deeply into her eyes. "I love listening to you speak. Your ideas are so refreshing. You see things, unfettered. Naively impossible, but refreshing."

"Naively impossible? I wonder why you seek my thoughts if you discount them so readily."

"No, you are not discounted. On the contrary, I'm desperately trying to imagine a time when I could throw my reputation to the wind and seek only my happiness." He shrugged. "It is the burden of being a duke to never truly consider such a thing."

"Then I pity every person of title, desperately grasping to rise higher and most jealously clinging to what little manner of elevation they've managed to gain through birth alone." She knew her words were fueled by the events of this morning, but she couldn't seem to stem the flow of words exiting her mouth.

But instead of being offended, the duke's eyes shown with admiration and he reached for her hand.

Warm thrills travelled up her arm from where he cradled her fingers in his palm. He turned over her hand and ran one finger from her wrist to the tip of her finger. "You are a fascination to me. The things you say, none of my acquaintance says. I would wager they've never considered. Thank you for listening, for saying such refreshing things. When I sit here with you, I feel as though I am free of societal restraint. And complex things in my life become clear. That is a gift." Her turned her hand over and brought her knuckle to his lips. They were soft, a velvety smooth pressure right on the back of her hand. She fought the urge to bring it up to her face afterward.

"Thank you."

Had she thanked a duke for kissing the back of her hand?

But he seemed not to notice her awkward reaction but only bowed his head and stood. "It is I who thank you."

She watched his retreating form until it disappeared into the darkness. Then she sat for many hours, staring after him, her mind on him and so many other things, she knew sleep would elude her. The one thought that struck in great waves of astonishment. Were she to present herself and come out for a season, there was the tiniest breath of a chance the duke could be hers. And that thought barreled through her with such a force, she imagined she'd never think another again.

Gerald wasn't sure how today was going to go. But he'd learned that in the case of Lady Rochester, he couldn't simply hand her off to the servants, but he must be involved personally. And her brother as well. Gerald's carriage arrived in front of her home. Her brother met him at the door.

"She is in the library. And thinks we are going on holiday to Brighton. With Your Grace."

"And she's not mistaken. Except for the part about me being involved much longer than dropping off and getting her situated. Hopefully she will be happy." Gerald adjusted his cravat.

"I imagine so. Most of the time. When she has her fits, the staff will be there to help manage, and when she's normal, she will have a lovely home and people to care for her." His eyes, full of sincerity, he turned to

Gerald. "Thank you. I cannot stomach dear Francis in Bedlam."

"Certainly. I have tenants nearby as well. Perhaps I'll engage them to simply be aware." The new family of sisters he'd inherited might be useful after all. He'd meet them today, after he left Lady Rochester.

Lady Rochester exited the house before they had stepped down from the carriage. And she seemed to be in the highest spirits. She even thanked the footman. Her brother seemed satisfied with the arrangement also. Gerald was much relieved. Even though he was strapped to an engagement that would never turn into a marriage, he had rid himself of being forced to marry such a woman. And she was far from his staff and most importantly, his son.

The journey was overly long and seemed laborious. Lady Rochester in a good mood almost grated on Gerald's nerves as much as the woman in a state of emotional fits. What had he been thinking, that he could marry a person and never see her? Not be a part of her life? He was obviously not thinking. His mouth turned in a small smile. Miss Amelia had been correct. He had needed time before he made any radical decisions.

They arrived at the house after what felt like a lifetime of travel. The house was quaint and in good repair, away from the major thoroughfare.

Lord Morley clapped his hands. "Oh, but this is lovely. Let's have a look inside, shall we?"

"Oh yes." Lady Rochester turned to Gerald. "I do think this quite appropriate. We both need some time away, I'd imagine, time to recover and accustom to things."

"Mm. Yes."

The housekeeper, Mrs. Lester, met them at the door. And as expected, she seemed on the larger side, more strong than anything. The footmen also. But everyone had an aura of goodness and one footman especially seemed cheerful even and willing to work to keep Lady Rochester happy. Gerald nodded. "Shall we sit in the front room?"

Lady Rochester nodded. "Yes, Mrs. Lester, could we have some tea brought?"

"Certainly."

The servants brought Lady Rochester's things upstairs while they sipped and talked of the good weather they had driving down.

Lady Rochester smiled and leaned back in her chair. "I don't imagine we'll need much at all here even as far as society. I find I'm quite pleased with the house."

Her brother smiled and squeezed her hand in his own. "I'm happy to hear it. And his grace has tenants who live nearby."

She wrinkled her nose.

"They're very well connected tenants, remember the distant family of the peerage, the very ones we were discussing."

"Ah, well good then. Perhaps I shall entertain them here."

"They might enjoy that, some superior attention would do them well." Her brother knew how to make Lady Rochester preen with self-importance, something Gerald could not abide.

He stood. "I think I shall go about the business of paying a call on my tenants, if you give me leave." He bowed.

They rose and curtseyed or bowed in return. "Would you like some company?" Lady Rochester's voice trailed away, and Gerald knew with relief that she had no desire to attend with him.

"No, I am perfectly happy to attend to matters of my estate." He bowed again and then exited the room and the home. He had no intention of returning. Her brother knew it. Lady Rochester did not. Hopefully she would be left in a stable, secure, and enjoyable situation.

The road opened up again as soon as he travelled further away from the cottage. And when he joined the main thoroughfare, he felt his breath coming easier. The sky was wide and blue and the air crisp with a coolness that soothed. He left some of the weight of his poor decisions and almost catastrophic move to marry someone of the likes of Lady Rochester, and began to hum with curiosity about this family of ladies.

He had written to expect him sometime this week. And when he pulled in, he was happily surprised to see staff and perhaps the ladies themselves standing on the front stoop to greet him. Their cottage sat just a small ways off the main thoroughfare. He'd heard that many a noble stopped to see them on their way to Brighton.

They were a lovely bunch, gifted with remarkable looks. Their dresses seemed worn but in the current style, their hair comely. Absolutely well-bred and of gentle birth. His footman opened the door, and when he stepped out and bowed, he was more than pleased at their elegant greeting in response.

He stepped forward. "And who do I have the pleasure of greeting? I am the Duke of Granbury."

The woman closest to him smiled at him and he was pleased to see good humor in her eyes. "Ah, the man so lucky to have inherited a dilapidated old castle and a family of sisters to go along with it?"

He coughed. "Well, I would never phrase it in such a manner."

Her eyebrow rose.

"But yes, you have the right of it."

A young girl stepped forward. "Have you seen the castle yet, Your Grace?" The youngest daughter seemed to be quite possibly not out of the school room. She might have been fourteen.

"I have not. I was hoping for a tour from you ladies?"

"Oh, absolutely. We'd love to, I'm sure." Her brazen expression and exuberant response made Gerald laugh, something he hadn't enjoyed in such a free manner in quite some time.

"And what is your name? You seem to be the adventurer of the family."

She curtseyed again. "I am Miss Grace. And they haven't allowed me to see the castle yet. I've not been at all, you see."

"Ah, and now you've seen an opportunity present itself?"

"Yes, Your Grace." Her smile was impish and proud. And Gerald decided he quite liked her.

His eyes returned to the first woman who spoke, Miss Standish. She held a hand out, indicating they move into the house. "Would you like to come in, refresh yourself and we can talk about the details of visiting such a place?"

"Such a place? Well, certainly. I would enjoy some tea and a rest in the cool of your front room." He followed them into the house. "And I've not been introduced to all of you."

When they were situated in a small but bright and cheery front room, Miss Standish did the honors of introductions to all four of her sisters. "Miss Charity, Miss Lucy, Miss Kate, Miss Grace, and of course, myself, Miss June Standish."

"And you are the relations of my departed cousin, relation to the Earl of Anglesey."

"We are."

"And he's not kept the castle in good repair."

"I'm afraid not, nor his estate, nor his affairs." Miss Kate muttered.

Gerald laughed. "Not too pleased with his handing you off in a will are you?"

A dark curly haired brunette dipped her head. "Forgive me, but would you be?"

Although the eldest shushed her, Gerald didn't imagine he'd be pleased, at all. "Well, let's see what we can do to make your lives a bit more enjoyable shall we?"

They seemed more pleased at that.

"And to begin, Miss Grace, I must go see this castle. You are welcome to join me, naturally."

"Oh if we must." Miss Standish winked at her younger sister, and Gerald decided he quite liked her as well.

"I'm full of curiosity to see why the place can be so loathsome. It has been in the hands of royal dukes for generations. It's quite a venerable past."

"Hmm." Was all the response he could muster from her.

They loaded into the carriage and were pressed for space, but none complained. "I'm certain one thing that might help every one of you would be more opportunities to attend events of the season. Surely Brighton offers much of a season, especially when Prinny is here."

They didn't respond which he found odd. Didn't every young lady long for a season, to flaunt her pretty self and find a husband? He'd determined this the most practical and helpful manner in which to aid these tenants.

As they drew closer to the castle, he lifted the fabric blocking the window and gazed at its massive size. "It's the largest home I've seen in many years."

They pulled up to the front, and as they all exited, he let the footman hand them down while he made his way slowly through the courtyard. They'd pulled in to a drive that was surrounded by half the castle. The walls towered up around him. After many minutes, some semblance of staff began to appear. Most seemed disheveled, all seemed uncaring. He'd have to fix that first of all. But he couldn't be putting too much money into the place, not unless he imagined some sort of return.

At great length, an older woman approached. When she curtseyed in front of them and looked like she might topple over, he suspected her being greatly in her cups. "Please show us to the main living area of the house, a sitting room or the like?"

She nodded and wobbled so much as she tried to walk in a straight line, that he said, "Oh, never mind, would you mind just pointing us in the correct direction?"

They moved together, weaving through old and drafty hallways, poorly lit rooms, everything covered in dirt and dust, until at last they found a cheery room with a fire, ancient tapestries lining the walls, sunlight shining in through larger windows.

"Ah, at last." He smiled.

They all took a seat. The youngest stood again rather rapidly. "Would anyone mind if I explored?"

"Yes." All her sisters answered at once.

She sat in a very slow and dejected manner which Gerald again found amusing.

When at last a maid entered the room, Gerald stood. "Would you please assemble all the staff?"

Her eyes widened but she nodded, curtseyed and left, her feet walking just slower than a run.

Gerald and Miss Standish worked together, interviewing the staff, talking about what areas needed work, in what ways the castle was livable, and by the end of his time there, he felt very much more positive about the whole of it. The other sisters had long been dismissed to take their own tour of the castle with a footman and maid in the midst of the interviews, and at last he and Miss Standish sat together, both keeping their thoughts to themselves.

"I must take my leave within the hour. But I have a favor to ask of you?" The longer he knew this woman, the more he respected her and all she was doing with her own sisters. Apparently they'd no parents left in the world, and no real family.

"Certainly. I'm grateful for all you're willing to do for the castle."

"Perhaps we can make it a livable situation, perhaps not. The cottage is cozy at any rate."

"Yes, very cozy." Her tone was never bitter, but Gerald got the impression she wished for more, and that their burden might be greater than she let on. He'd have his steward look into their finances and expenses once he returned.

"I have a situation here in a cottage close to you."

Her wrinkled nose made him smile. "You know, you look just like my best friend. You'd enjoy him..." His mouth lifted in a smile larger than he had planned but he kept the rest of his thoughts to himself.

"At any rate, we've recently relocated my fiancé to a cottage near you." He told her all the details of his and Lady Rochester's arrangements. He was open and honest and when he'd finished, she said, "And now you are forever engaged?"

"It appears so."

She pressed her lips together obviously not saying some thought or other that was pressing on her mouth to be freed.

"Every now and then, could you look into her situation? If you don't wish to visit, because we aren't sure how she will respond to her new solitary life, at least ask the servants to check in with theirs? I will alert them that you are a trusted household."

She nodded. "Of course. We'll pay a visit straight away."

"For that I thank you."

The other sisters arrived, and their group left the castle with plans to hire a new housekeeper, add to the staff, and begin work on the main living areas. When Gerald dropped the women off at their cottage with promises of more and better things to come, he felt quite good about the manner in which he would be leaving things. And he wondered suddenly if Miss Amelia would agree.

He settled back into his carriage seat and thought of her. Their last meeting had intrigued him. He'd felt the tiniest spark of interest, a hint of attraction, and a great amount of respect. If he must marry again, why could he not choose someone who he got on well with?

His chest tightened. But of course he couldn't marry Miss Amelia. His mother would begin an apoplexy the likes of which no one had seen. Had she not warned him against such a thing, called it a Marguerite or something. He closed his eyes, imagining Miss Amelia's face. Well, he could at least try to find someone like her, someone who could comfort and guide him through many lonely days ahead. Up until this moment, tender thoughts of any other woman had felt surely to be a betrayal to his beloved Camilla. But now, since he'd met his son, he knew his heart was opening to the possibility of a happy life, and the more he thought about it, the more he suspected that Camilla would approve.

THE NEXT DAY, GERALD FOUND HIS WAY TO THE park across the street from his home. It was early in the morning and just as he hoped, no one else was about.

The birds were especially loud and were it not for Camilla's great fondness for birds, he would have been quite cross with the creatures.

He walked further into the park toward his favorite location. He'd come often when thinking through his young concerns, when trying to consider whether to ask for Camilla's hand, when pondering particularly trying situations in the House of Lords. In fact, it seemed remarkable to him that he hadn't come to the park even in the dark of night, the night he turned instead to the tea shop. Fate had a hand, certainly.

As he entered the hedgerows that his a fountain and arbor at their center, he was surprised and disappointed at a hint of movement inside. But as he made his way deeper into the hedgerows, his heart warmed with happiness. Miss Amelia.

"Just the person I hoped to see."

She jumped and covered her mouth with one gloved hand.

Uncanny to him how she seemed to act so far above her station. Then she curtseyed as if to further prove the truth of his thoughts and said, "Your Grace." Her smiled grew. "And how are you this early morning? I admit to pondering over you in just this moment. You left in such a hurry the other evening."

"I did, didn't I? Well, I shall tell you all. But today is not the day for that. Today, I should just like to pretend that all is right in the world and that you and I are having an enjoyable meander in the park." He held out his arm.

When she placed her hand at the crook of his elbow, he was astounded at the peace that filled him. He nodded. "Just so."

They did not say much. He did not wish to elaborate on his doings in Brighton, not yet. As he made his way through a part of the park he'd not shared with many, some significant parts of his life seemed to shift into better focus and he could only attribute his greater clarity to time spent with the remarkable Miss Amelia.

❧ 12 ❧

All the dresses had come back from the modiste. All the countless pieces of clothing that Amelia had no idea were essential parts of a lady's costume had filled her room at home and her new room at her grandparents' house. She'd had one visit with a dance instructor, and he found her so proficient no more were needed. Amelia was grateful for his tips on the typical country dance sets the ladies chose. He rehearsed with her different forms of the Quadrille and refreshed her knowledge of the Waltz. Her grandmother reviewed forms of address for different people of title and found her wonderfully prepared and knowledgeable. "I would expect nothing less of you with such a mother."

Amelia beamed with pride in her mother. And all at once, all those years of lessons seemed to be precious time and knowledge. Amelia stood with her grandmother's favorite dress flowing down all around her as though all of those years were in preparation for this moment. It was lavender. The bright white lace lined the bottom of the gown, the sleeves and also added embellishment to the ribbon around her waist. And Amelia loved it. Mostly because one of her mother's dresses in her trunk was the same shade of lavender.

"You look lovely. You're going to send everyone into fits, trying to meet you."

Amelia laughed. "Well, I don't know if I want them in fits."

"I do."

Amelia laughed again. She had no idea that her at first stern grandmother could be such a delight.

"If they aren't in fits, I'll be shocked and amazed." Her grandfather winked and entered, holding out his hands.

She placed her own in his palms. "Grandfather."

"You look lovely."

"Thank you. This is all so incredible. I didn't fancy myself much of a dreamer, but I admit I have never been more excited."

"Excellent. We are perhaps even more excited to finally share our granddaughter with all our friends."

"I hope I do you justice."

"My dear, we couldn't be prouder."

The warmth that spread at their declaration made Amelia so happy and filled her with much needed confidence. She was excited for new introductions, for the opportunity to make her way among the peerage who she so often served, but more than anything, she hoped that a certain duke would be present. She didn't dare ask her grandparents. How silly for her to even imagine she'd be a notable person in the duke's life. But even if she could just see him, she would be partly satisfied. If he could see her, dressed like she belonged in his world, she would be even more satisfied and perhaps, if he turned to look twice, she'd have satisfied all her secret wishes.

They climbed into the carriage, and Amelia tried very hard not to fidget. Her grandmother seemed to have no trouble at all sitting still.

"Years of practice."

"Pardon?"

"I can see you are so full of energy it wants to burst out of you. You will not believe it, but I feel the same."

Her stately frame appeared to be in the perfect state of repose. "Try it."

Amelia studied her. "I'm not sure I can accomplish such a thing." But she imitated her grandmother's exact pose, stared off into space, and let her air out slowly.

"There, you've done it."

"Have I?" She whispered. "I even feel more relaxed, a thing I thought impossible."

'The two of you look as though you will become statues long before we arrive." Her grandfather chuckled.

Amelia grinned at them both. "I believe I can do this."

"Now, remember what we are telling everyone."

"Yes, the truth. You have just discovered me after all these years."

"I wish we could say simply that you have been away, and leave it at that."

"Except most of these ladies have at least seen me in the shop. Whether or not they recognize me as the same person is yet to be seen. But if even one of them does..."

"Say no more. We are owning up to the truth before they can." Her grandmother waved her hand. "All shall be well. We've some important people who support you as well as one of the Patronesses who is, I admit, mostly curious and caught up in the romance of your situation."

"Romance?"

"The romance she imagines is sure to come."

"Hmm."

They stepped out of the carriage and made their way into a grand home, climbed the stairs and were soon standing at the entrance to a ball room, decorated in flowers and all manner of candles. Amelia stood regally, ready to be announced.

She watched the swirling dancers grateful she was not the most finely dressed woman in the room. Though earlier, as soon as she saw her dress, she'd thought that surely she would be, having never seen anything so fine. But knowing that attention would be drawn in other directions made her feel better immediately.

As soon as she and the Baron and his wife were announced, several groups of people came forward at once. And the Baron was introducing his grand-daughter to all and sundry. Amelia felt immediately lost in a sea of faces she was meant to remember. But soon a man asked her for the next dance which was just beginning and whisked her off to the floor.

He bowed. "I am sorry to pull you away so soon from all those that would meet you."

"Oh, I'm grateful. I don't know if I'll remember even three of their names."

"I myself have a difficulty remembering names."

"Oh, good, I mean, it's not good you forget names, just that I feel better knowing someone else shares my weakness." She winced. "Not that yours is a weakness."

He started to laugh. "You are amusing. You act as though this is your first ball."

"Oh, well—"

Their dance began and she was spared the burden of concocting something witty to say. She watched the first couple to remind herself what must be done, and then she and her partner circled the others, circled each other and then returned to their place in line. She studied the face of her partner, Lord Herring. He was certainly handsome. And a titled lord of some kind. Before she met the Duke she might have been completely tongue tied, worse than she was, because of the man's status in life. But now, she compared the two and found this new lord wanting. His eyes didn't hold hers with burning sincerity. His hair was not as brilliant or thick. His nose rather small. She shook her head, laughing at her own ridiculous thoughts. As if a nose is a measure of a man.

Her gaze travelled around the room, while her partner danced across from her and just before it was her turn, her eyes caught the duke's.

She sucked in a breath and almost missed her steps, knowing he was watching. What would he think? Was he astonished to see a shopkeeper here at the ball? Did he notice her finery? She performed the steps with exactness and energy.

Lord Herring nodded. "You're quite the proficient."

"Thank you." The smile she gifted him was in hopes that the duke would see. They continued on, making small talk about everything from the latest gossip of which she even knew a little from the conversations at the tea shop, to the weather, to the upcoming activities of the week. She thought a dance had never lasted as long as this one when it finally ended and they clapped in gratitude.

Lord Herring would have escorted her from the floor, but as she lifted her fingers to rest on his arm, the duke swept in and reached for her hand. He held hers firmly in his own and bowed over her hand. "Miss Amelia. It is a pleasure to see you again. I believe I have this dance?"

"Oh, well."

He lead her away. And the music for the waltz began.

"Was this meant to be a waltz?" She had checked the order and the music, hoping to prepare. "And honestly, you did not have this dance."

"I requested a change." He smirked. "And whoever I've stolen you away from will be all the more anxious to gain your attention again when we're through." He held himself almost regally. The power from his broad shoulders, his raised chin, the fire dancing in his eyes was intoxicating. She tried to maintain a certain level of respectability but inside she thought she might at last really and truly swoon.

She raised her eyebrows. "You wanted to dance a waltz with me?"

His eyes shown with what looked like possible interest, but then he said. "I assumed this the simplest manner in which to have a private conversation. I've asked for the longest waltz ever made."

She laughed, partly disappointed, but also put well and truly at ease by his returning to their usual manner together.

"I have news. But first, I must tell you. You look amazing. Beautiful. And I must know. How are you here?"

She tipped her head to the Baron and his wife who were standing at attention watching their every move. "Have you met my grandparents?"

His face filled with a happy sort of delight. "Lord Smithson?"

"Yes, the very one."

"Why he's the most revered fellow. Most here hold him in the highest regard."

"I'm pleased to hear it. I've recently become reacquainted with them, and they wished that I attend."

"And now the desire to know you has increased tenfold. For I sense a rather involved story."

"Yes, well, come by the tea shop any time. Or you may come calling at my grandparents' home." She hoped to remind him she had no pretense. Though she knew if she went to the tea shop, it would be to visit her father, or as a customer only.

He shook his head. "I don't believe I've ever had a conversation that will be a unique as this one is bound to be. "So, I have to tell you the details of my week past."

"What has happened?" She was happy to see more energy in his face, more excitement to live.

"I have sent Lady Rochester to live in a cottage by herself."

"So it's been done." Her voice came out overly loud, and she glanced around to see most of the room was already overly interested in her waltz with the duke. She tried to ignore them.

"Her brother went with me. It is the best thing. After the fuss she made out on the street, the family was considering bedlam."

"Oh my, oh dear."

"Yes, and I'm particularly pleased because as you know, I should have listened to you in the first place but since I didn't I was rather tied to her in marriage. And when I met my son." He tipped his head back. "It's been so long I didn't tell you. I met. My. Son." His eyes shone with moisture now and she couldn't breathe for the beautiful image of a father in love with his son.

"I'm so happy for you. Is he as handsome as—" She gasped. "Oh my. What I mean to say..." She laughed at his raised eyebrows. "Well, alright. Is he as handsome as his father?" She wanted to hide behind the nearest pillar, sure her cheeks were flaming as red as they felt hot.

"I believe he has surpassed me already. And I must tell you, for you have become the person I tell all the very private emotional dealings of my heart. He looks like his mother."

She swallowed. Did he hear himself? What was he saying to her? "Camilla?" she bit her cheek, "I mean, the duchess?"

"Yes, and I didn't want to see it. I was afraid. I admit it. I was afraid of.." He swallowed twice, and Amelia wished to change the subject to spare him the telling.

"Of the pain." She understood.

He nodded and stretched his neck against his cravat. Then cleared his throat twice before continuing. "And obviously I'm still aching like my heart might fall out of my chest. But." He rotated his shoulders under her hand and she was amazed at the power there, the rippling of the muscles through his jacket. "But when I saw her nose, and the set of her lips on my own son, I could only smile. Grateful" He exhaled in one long slow breath. "There, that was more difficult to get out than I thought it would be."

She pressed her fingers into his shoulder, applying more pressure there. "I'm so incredibly happy for you. On all counts. Things are looking up. And might I say, it's perfectly acceptable to be afraid, sad, or happy. For that is how we are made."

He was quiet for a long time as they glided across the floor. And then he said. "I think I fear happiness most of all."

Her own eyes misted. "Yes. That's a long-lived fear in me."

He searched her face. Their eyes communicating understanding and words that would never need to be spoken. Then he surprised her and spun her around, double beat to the waltz.

She laughed louder than she meant to and then gasped. "Oh, you're an excellent dancer."

"And so are you." He pulled her closer than even the waltz allowed. "And might I know how you come to be so accomplished, so well spoken, such a comfortable dance partner, knowing the waltz no less, and fitting so well here in a London society ball?"

She shrugged. "My mother." Then laughed. "But I have half a mind to remind ye I ken mop up the floors almost as well."

His laugh made her grin. "And do you dance with the broom?"

She looked away. "Perhaps."

"So how do I compare?"

"With a broom?"

"Well, yes, I assume it was your most common dance partner?"

"It was not my only dance partner and I will admit you compare very favorably."

"To your other partners?"

"To my broom."

"Ha ha!" He looked around and she noticed almost every eye on them. "Shall we take a stroll outside in the gardens?"

"Dare we?"

"I always dare."

She lifted her chin. "Then I do as well. Do you think my grandparents will approve?"

"Of you spending time with a duke?" His eyebrow rose like only a completely confident duke's could.

She shrugged. "Then let's go."

He placed her hand on his arm and practically ran as he led her from the room. They raced out to the verandah and then down the stairs and out in the well-lit gardens. Many other couples were walking slowly along the paths. That relieved Amelia somewhat, not wanting to create scandal at her very first appearance in society. She and the duke would not be alone. But they could speak in private, and she enjoyed that thought most of all.

They meandered along in comfortable silence for a moment, the smell of roses filling the air around them, making her smile and breathe deeply.

"You like roses."

Pleased he'd noticed, she nodded. "I do. And these are particularly lovely." The arbors, marking entrances to smaller gardens carried cascading flowers of all different colors. The night air felt cool on her skin that was unaccountably warm in the duke's presence.

The stars twinkled far above, and the moon and candles and torches lit the area. She'd not seen anywhere quite so magical ever, and she recognized she was in danger of being swept away by her reaction to it all and by the handsome man at her side. Who, she tried to remind herself, was not interested in her or anyone right now. He sought her company as a good sounding board, a person wholly unrelated to him whom he could confide in. She caught his eyes, reflecting the flickering light from a torch, smiling at her, and she knew, she was in danger in deed.

He searched her face and then looked away. "I thought it wouldn't matter if I remained engaged forever. I was no longer looking for a wife, Lady Rochester well and truly cured me of that desire..." He turned to her with questioning eyes. "But now I don't know..."

"Are you asking if you should be seeking a wife?"

"No, well, perhaps. I don't know. I don't trust myself to know any more. I thought for certain that marriage to a woman like Lady Rochester would take away all my cares." He grimaced. "I've never been so wrong, but you, you were right, and Lord Morley, he was right too. Before Camilla died, I never had reason to question my own judgment always relying on it like an old friend, but now, I don't know." He stopped. When she looked up into his face, she noticed how surprisingly close he stood. And she found it hard to breathe, particularly difficult to think.

"What is it you want to know?"

He stepped closer, and her heart raced. Would she be able to answer him at all? She didn't know.

"I wonder if perhaps my idea of finding a wife might not have been so bad afterall, if I found the right woman." He lifted a hand to brush the hair out of her face, leaving a trail of sensations along her skin she'd never felt before. She couldn't breathe. Everything around them went silent and the longer she looked into his eyes, the further away from reality she drifted. The duke, marriage..then her thoughts stuttered. Marriage. He had just lost his wife six months past. He was in no position to fall in love.

He stepped back. "Forgive me. My thoughts drifted to places they should not go at the moment." His pause was more a question than a silence, his eyebrows raised. "Should they?"

She forced herself to make a noise, cleared her throat. "Perhaps, someday, our thoughts could go places?" What had she just said! Words were exiting her lips without any thought involved. She needed to run, or walk, or crawl away from this man, return to her grandparents and dance with more accessible, reasonable choices.

"Do you think that we might, converse, now and then?"

"I'd enjoy that."

"Would your father or your grandfather like to talk about my intentions? I am very much engaged. I want to make certain I am clear of any other obligations naturally. If such a thing would be possible."

A thrill coursed through her and a smile grew on her face before she could stop it. "I'm certain that both would like to have that conversation when you are ready."

He reached for her hand and entwined their fingers. "I don't know much of anything right now. I don't trust my judgement or my heart, but I find the thought of time with you brings a certain peace and stability I only find with Morley. And he's not as pleasing to look upon, and he lacks a certain appeal, and he'll be getting married sometime. I hope for his own happiness.

"I didn't think I could ever really hope for a continued relationship with you, but when I saw you here, dancing, looking more beautiful than any other woman in the room, something changed inside and instead of feeling hopelessly lonely, a tiny door opened the inkling of a thought that maybe one day, I could be happy again, that I could enjoy a new relationship, not like the one I had with Camilla but a new one that fills the deep loneliness with something, and offers a family and a mother for my son." He took a breath and then his eyes filled with alarm. He stepped back.

"What is it?"

"I can't believe I said all of that. Are, are you well?"

"I-I hardly know."

"Again, I apologize. I'm in no position to be talking about anything at all. I'm betrothed to another."

She reached for him and rested a hand on his arm. "I'm happy you did."

"And would you, could you be amendable to talks?" He waved his hands in front of his face. "Just talks."

"Always."

He nodded. "Talks. Excellent."

"Should we return inside?"

"Yes, let's return you to your grandparents. And might I plan to call on you tomorrow?"

"Yes, I'd like that." Could a person marry someone other than their soul match and still be happy? She imagined so for some, but at this moment, walking on the arm of the Duke of Granbury, she knew down to her toes, she could be happy with no one else.

❧ 13 ❧

The duke hurried through his ministrations with the valet. He impatiently swatted away the man's extra efforts on his cravat and then hurried out the door, calling to the staff that he would not need the carriage.

They were to meet at the tea shop, which, though very close, seemed impossibly far this afternoon. Every step took a thousand moments. His feet couldn't move fast enough. And Gerald needed to see Miss Amelia. He'd thought of nothing else since his dance with her. He hadn't been so fixated on another person since...He couldn't think it, couldn't say the name in his mind. Such a strong feeling of betrayal filled him he wasn't sure. Could he feel, interest, in another? Was he allowed that bit of hope?

He stepped up to the door and to his surprise, the shop was full, not a corner free for anyone, not for him especially. Unfortunately many eyes in the room turned to him, standing with his face peering in the door window.

Nothing for it but to step inside. The chatter hushed and many hopeful female eyes turned to look at him. Dash it all, where were the men?

Then a pair of eyes and a large smile at the back peered up over the heads of everyone else. Lord Morley.

"Praise be," He muttered as he made his way to the back, most of the ladies, tittered and giggled and fanned their faces at him.

Then to his left an evil laugh twisted inside him in a painful wrench and before he could turn his head, the sound of a tea cup crashing to the ground made him wince. "How dare you dump tea on me, pick that up. We'll not come if we are to be stained by the help."

Gerald turned to see Amelia stooping at the feet of Lady Pallin, picking up shards of ceramic from the floor, tea staining her own skirts. He hurried to peer around the corner and saw what he hoped was waiting for him. A broom.

"Allow me?" He held the broom out.

Several gasps echoed in the room and Amelia shook her head. "Oh no. Your Grace. Let me." While they worked, she murmured. "Father needed help. When I got here, this crowd was too much for him and the assistant." Her eyes shone with gratitude, but he knew she was mortified at his actions.

"I insist. If you'll show me how it's done?"

The rest of the shop stared in amazement while the two of them cleaned up the tea service that had been broken all over the floor. Then they carried the pieces to the back.

As soon as they rounded the corner, Amelia whispered. "What are you doing?"

"I cannot abide those women. How can they possibly think themselves above someone like you?"

Her face turned bright red and she tried to hide her smile before she said. "But I need friends. Lady friends, or I'll never make it."

"I don't see how that signifies at all. As if you need the likes of them. We'll find you the sort of friends you need."

She eyed him as though he'd said something strange but she did not respond. Instead, she curtseyed and made to return to the main tea room.

"Wait, what are you doing?"

"My job." Her eyes were full of challenge. "Or have you forgotten that I am a shopkeeper's daughter. I serve the likes of those women every day."

"But you don't have to, your grandparents..."

"Cannot erase my parentage. Who, might I add, I am immensely proud of."

She placed a hand on his sleeve. "My father needs help, but I see how this might prevent my having a, shall we say, advantageous alliance or even friendship?"

"Friendship, no, Miss Amelia..."

She shook her head and hurried back to the tea room main room.

The duke was left to mumble after her, "I'll see you later tonight to talk more about that."

He left the tea shop with Lord Morley. His friend eyed him with the strangest expression and then he said, "What precisely are you doing, pursuing the shopkeeper's daughter?"

"That's not all she is—and I don't know. I find I have a desperate need to talk to her. And be near her. It's the strangest thing. For all this while I miss Camilla like I would miss my arm, my leg, half my heart. Yet this Miss Amelia seems to hold a place as well. I think. I don't even know."

"I think you better figure it out before you leap into any more rash decisions. And while you're at it, figure out what you plan to do about Lady Rochester. You cannot possibly think to stay engaged to her forever."

"I would not be able to bear it."

"Then what are you going to do?"

"I hardly know." He laughed, half-heartedly, but I'll tell you the first person I wish to consult?"

"Miss Amelia."

"Precisely. And that knowledge tells me something."

"Then I say you do so."

"You could come."

"What, while you woo the shopkeepers' daughter?"

"Those aren't the words I would use, but, yes."

"Wouldn't miss it."

"Tonight after closing."

"Perhaps that would be better, to keep things on the up and up, now that I know she's the Baron Smithson's granddaughter."

"She's who?"

"The very one. And looks even more amazing in a ballgown."

"I imagine so."

"You do?"

"Certainly."

When the duke narrowed his eyes, he added, "perhaps not so far as imagining her in a ballgown, just that she's lovely. And would be lovelier still dressed up for a ball?"

"Ah yes, precisely that."

They spent the early evening hours together and then made their way back to the tea shop just after closing.

"Come, let's help her clean up."

"What has come over you? As if you know how to clean anything."

"It cannot be that difficult."

They stepped inside the shop, and Miss Amelia waved them in her face coloring in an enchanting manner. "I'll just be a moment."

A knock at the door startled them both. A rider entered and bowed. "The Duke of Granbury?"

"Yes, here."

"Express from Miss Standish of Gayhurst cottage."

"My tenants. Outside of Brighton." He took it and paid the rider. "Please wait a moment in case a response is required." He broke the seal and skimmed the contents. Then gripped his friend's arm. "This changes everything." He clutched the letter in his hand. "I must be away."

He ran for the door, determined to be on his horse now.

"Dash it all, Gerald. Wait. What is this about?" Lord Morley's voice faded away as Gerald ran down the streets towards his home.

...

Amelia watched two of the most eligible men in the ton run as though chased by a ghost down the street and away from her store. As soon as they were out of sight, she slumped against the table. A day to return to serving in the shop to help her father had turned into the most tiresome of any in her recent past. Never had she resented serving the ladies of the ton as much as she had today, never had they been so cruel.

She didn't understand much of anything right then, but she clung to some of her strongest thoughts. The experiment to attempt to present her as a member of the upper classes in London was not going to work. Unfortunately, her unexplainable closeness to the Duke of Granbury was only complicating matters. And she didn't know if her tea shop would survive this new bout of persecution. For the first time ever, she didn't know if she wanted it to. As yet, her father was unaware of the negativity but she couldn't bear to let him find out. Perhaps it was time to move out, to their house in the country.

❧ 14 ❧

Gerald and Lord Morley rode through the night and holed up in a nearby Inn. When their valets had left them for the night, Lord Morley shook his head. "And you're saying she's been seeing the footman?"

"For many years. Apparently, all through her previous marriage. They fell in love or some other such thing, and there you have it."

"And what do you plan to do about it?"

"Confront her. Explain her options."

Morley held his hand out in question. "Which are?"

"Well the way I see it, I need her to back away from this engagement."

"You think she'll agree to do so."

"It's likely, when confronted with the alternative which includes making all and sundry aware of her indiscretions."

Morley's grin started slow and then grew. "Seems a persuasive motivation."

"I'm confident she will see things my way."

"How did you come to know the details?"

"This family of sisters. They are my new tenants. Have we discussed them?"

"No." Morley frowned. "What have they to do with this?"

"I asked them to keep an eye on things for me, and they have apparently, remarkably well. They're quite plucky, all of them. I think you'll enjoy meeting them."

"Will we go there first?"

"Yes, in addition to my desire that you meet them, I wish to clarify the story and make certain I proceed appropriately."

"Wise." He cleared his throat. "Should I be concerned that you seem to have a particular desire that I meet them?"

"Not at all." Gerald smiled to himself. Making his friend the happiest of men while at the same time ridding himself of one of the sisters would be just the thing. "You know, they're very well connected. As far as tenants go, I've acquired some of the best. Pleasing to look upon and friends with the Duke of Norfolk, did I tell you?"

Lord Morley did not answer but Gerald wasn't concerned. He'd soon see for himself.

They arrived at the front door earlier than was typical for callers, but Gerald gave the hour no mind. He was lost in a new hope that involved Amelia in his life. In what manner he had not yet decided, but he knew that it had become vital to his well-being that she be a part of whatever future plans he might have.

The ladies were all up and dressed, remarkably, and greeted him at the door. Miss Standish stepped forward. "Oh, you came quickly. I imagine so, the situation being what it is."

Miss Grace leaned forward. And Gerald cleared his throat. "Perhaps we might converse in private?"

"Oh, certainly." Her face colored a little.

"We can ask a maid to attend, or better yet, Lord Morley, would you join us?"

He started, but then recovered and said, "Certainly. Lead the way."

Gerald felt the eyes of the sisters on his back as they made their way to the study. In truth, he didn't need to discuss much with Miss Standish. But he did enjoy seeing his friend discomfited. For the ladies were, each of them, some of the most beautiful he'd seen.

When they were situated and the door shut, Gerald leaned forward. "I thank you for your timely express.

You cannot know how very fortunate I feel in having received your news."

She nodded, waiting.

"I'd like to ascertain how you came by the information and to know if there have been further developments?"

"We stopped by the first day to pay a social call, as I said we would."

"Thank you."

"And I noticed on that visit that something was odd about this particular footman. He seemed far too familiar with Lady Rochester, but also with us. The servants of course were asked to discover what they could. And all of us were of the same opinion that something about him was simply off." She looked out the window. "I do not wish to speak so plainly and so ill of another, but I happened upon them in the garden and they were..." She looked away. "in an embrace."

"Unbelievable." Lord Morley grimaced. "And I do apologize that yours must be the eyes to witness such a scene."

"Oh, thank you. I feel it is the least we can do to help when the duke has been so kind."

She shook her head. "I must continue this sordid tale. For the servants then inquired and one became more of a friend to their footman." She shrugged. "It was he that revealed the history between himself and Lady Rochester."

"The embrace is proof enough, but the tale from his own lips only helps strengthen my own relief of conscience that ending our betrothal might in some way harm her."

"You can rest assured that I don't even believe her to be mentally incapable. I suspect her to have contrived such a situation, that all of her emotional distress was but a facade."

Gerald gritted his teeth in annoyance. "So that she might carry on with her footman in privacy? With no pressure from her brother to remarry?" Did she even merit a visit from him? He thought not. "Perhaps I shall write her a letter detailing our new terms. How can I abide to look upon her, hearing her true nature revealed?"

"But to hear her agreement to your terms. I think you must."

"So be it." He noticed an increasing amount of glances between the two of them, so he made his way to the door. "If you could spare a footman, I shall leave you to it, go and return without anyone further encumbered."

"What? Surely you'd like some company?"

"No, a footman will suffice."

Lord Morley eyed him as if he'd grown an extra set of arms, but he stayed with Lady Standish, and Gerald hurried to the home of Lady Rochester, his own cottage, to deliver his terms.

❧ 15 ❧

Perhaps Amelia had been a bit rash in her decision to run from London. But who could blame her? The duke had disappeared for days. The mistreatment by the lady customers persisted, and her father could tell something was amiss. Her grandparents had written many a letter inviting her to stay, alerting her of coming engagements, but she'd answered none of them.

And now, sitting on the front porch to their charming house in the country, she could only feel a twinge of guilt. She and her father were happy in the country. At least she told herself so. They'd saved money, and something she hadn't known, her mother had a substantial dowry that her father had been keeping for Amelia to use when the time came. And from it, they were able to have a small income, if they chose.

Her father resisted the notion, but she insisted, at least for the time. They could sell the London shop and purchase one far away from there, perhaps even near their cottage. She told herself she was content, if not happy even; but she could never be so, not with things left unsettled the way they were, not knowing she'd never see the duke just happen upon her one evening. Was she running away? Certainly. She preferred the quiet real conversations of the shop owners and working class who she was raised knowing. The duke had that same sincerity, goodness, his friend, Lord Morley also. Perhaps there were members of the ton she could admire and enjoy. Her grandparents were lovely. She stood. "I believe I need a good walk about the grounds. We've no idea if the fences are well and mended."

"Don't be long. Would you like to bring Jasper?"

Their dog belonged to the house. They asked the maid to feed it while they were away. They weren't sure how it happened upon them but allowed him to finish out his days in his home. "I don't think he'd make it."

Her father chuckled. And she waved to him as she rounded the back of the house. The further she walked out into the open fields, the easier she breathed, the freer she felt and a certain boldness overtook her. "And why can't I be happy?"

Horse hooves sounded behind her. She whipped around, startled. A man, a gentleman, rode a tan horse with a black mane, white socks on his two front legs. She couldn't make out much else but curiosity rose up to the surface, and she waited while the newcomer rode closer. But the more she studied him, something familiar jogged her mind and her heart skipped when she recognized a certain tilt of the head. The rider made his way closer and the sound of his laugh rose like a wave inside, racing through her in a crazed crashing of white frothy happiness. "What!" she waved her arm.

He at last skidded to stop in front of her, leaping from his horse and rushing to her.

She wasn't sure what to expect, from his actions she thought for certain he would pick her up and spin her around in his arms, but at the moment such an action would have been expected, he stopped in an awkward lurch and held out his hand, "Miss Amelia."

He placed her hand in his. He bowed over it, allowing his lips to linger on her knuckles for the briefest of moments. Or had she imagined it?

"Your grace. What..."

"I've come. I mean. I found you. You left." His accusing eyes made her look away.

"I—" Her words came out breathless. "I thought it for the best."

"You did?" He tipped his head. "That cannot be so. For how could being apart from someone so linked to your very soul be a wise move?"

She gasped. "You've felt it too?"

"Most certainly. How could it be otherwise? I know I come with a partly broken heart so what I offer might not be whole." He paused.

She watched him. "What you offer?" Hope refused to lighten the way, for now.

"Yes, Amelia, oh my lovely Amelia, somehow this broken heart still functions. And it has learned how to love again. For I love you. And I cannot imagine my life without you. I thought perhaps visiting you at the tea room might suffice, but that's an awful manner in which to spend time with the one you love. And besides, you'd left."

She refused to acknowledge the joy that was trying to overflow into her common sense. "And what about Lady Rochester?"

"She's gone. She's recanted all of her previous nonsense, and broken off our engagement... Which brings me to my offer. He lowered himself to one knee. "Miss Amelia Dickson, I am quite without a duchess, and a mother to my son..."

Her heart pinched in a touch of sorrow. Is that all he wanted from her? What he'd hoped from Lady Rochester?

He held up his finger. "And my soul longs for its missing part, which I found in you. I love you. When I thought I could never love again, I discovered the heart's infinite capacity to love. And now I cannot even recognize my life without you in it. Please, my dear Amelia, consent to be my wife."

She stepped closer. Could they make a happy life together? "What would happen if I did this?" She stood as close as she could, as close as she dared. Then reached up to run a hand down the side of his face. He closed his eyes and the smile of enjoyment encouraged her.

He wrapped an arm around her back and stood, their faces close. "Or this."

She reached her hands up to his shoulders, loving the feeling of his arms around her. But uncertain how he would respond, knowing that she shared moments like this one with ghosts of his first wife. She stood on tiptoe. "I wonder how you would feel about..." As her lips moved closer to Gerald's, he surprised her and closed the distance immediately, covering hers with his own. Warmth and happiness filled her, a sense of completion and wonder raced from her head to her toes, while his mouth explored hers in a growing intensity. She pulled him tighter. Could it be? Was he free to love again? Could they have a happy marriage?

He kissed her again and again. And then, when he paused for a moment, his mouth still hovering near hers, he repeated, "I love you Amelia. I can't believe it is so, but I love you and want you to be my wife." He pressed his forehead against hers and waited, with eyes closed.

"Gerald?"

He opened his eyes.

"Yes. I love you too. I have from the moment I first met you."

His smile grew and he kissed her once more on the lips, then the nose, then the forehead. "You've made me the happiest of men. Can this really be so?"

It was most definitely...so.

EPILOGUE

Gerald pulled his wife closer, the waltz his most requested dance of late.

"Isn't such a thing scandalous?" Amelia raised an eyebrow in pretend dismay as only she could.

"If I can't create a little scandal with my own wife then I don't know what more to do for these people."

"I guess scandal with one's wife is appropriate? Yes?"

"Of course it depends entirely on who's speaking, but I will always find any activity with you appropriate no matter what anyone says." A protective warmth filled him as he watched the light dance in his wife's eyes. His arms circled about her more closely and he moved them to the more secluded parts of the ballroom floor.

She melted into him. "I love it when you hold me like this."

"Like I can't be close enough?"

"Well, yes." Her reddening cheeks warmed him all the more. "But more as if this dance were an embrace."

Pleased, he searched her face. "And so it is. And now, all this talk of closeness, scandal and embraces makes me think we should pay a visit upstairs."

Amelia gasped and looked around.

"To visit our son."

"Oh you are too much. Such a tease."

"And if I kiss you on the stairs, so be it." He danced them to the rear of the room where an exit would allow them easy access to a back stairwell. Once they'd slipped from the room, he pulled her close, "Or here. We could even take a small break and I could kiss you right here."

A small gasp interrupted and a maid hurried past, fighting a smile.

"Look what you've done."

"What? More scandal with my own wife? I thought we'd covered this."

"Oh, all right. Let's have some of that scandal, then." She moved closer.

"Now we're talking."

After thoroughly kissing his wife, he tugged her hand and they raced upstairs and into the nursery.

"Father!" Richard raced to Gerald and was swung up into the air. Then Richard pulled on Amelia's hand. "Mother come see." Gerald winked at her upturned face and then watched as his son showed Amelia his work in the school room. Gerald had worried about how he'd feel when his son called Amelia mother. What would Camilla think? But as he looked up at her smiling portrait, he couldn't help but think she'd be pleased.

Amelia came to stand beside him, and he pulled her closer once more. " I love you my wife."

"I love you too."

***

Read on for the introduction to Lord Morley's story, Book Two, The Earl's Winning Wager.

THE EARL'S WINNING
WAGER

Morley stared at his best friend, waiting for the man to look up from his cards. Gerald was losing terribly. And Morley wasn't sure if he should feel guilty or victorious. His friend had just thrown most of a new inheritance from his distant cousin on the table, almost as if he wished to give it away.

Despite Gerald being the Duke of Granbury with significant holdings to his name, Morley wasn't comfortable taking so much—even in something as unbiased as a card game. But his friend smiled so large it looked like his cheeks hurt. Morley's hurt just looking at him.

"How can you smile when you're losing abominably?" Lord Morley frowned at him.

"I have leave to be happy so soon after my own wedding."

"But you don't have leave to gamble away your living, even to your best friend."

"I'm hardly close to losing a living."

Lord Morley raised his eyebrows. The other lords at the table stared greedily at the back of Gerald's cards. But even though Lord Morley shook his head, none too subtly, Gerald pushed all the remaining chips and his slips of paper into the center.

"Included in this are some holdings in the south."

Lord Morley narrowed his eyes.

Gerald fanned out his cards. "Good, but"—he smiled even broader—"not good enough." Then each of the men laid out their cards. Gerald beat Lord Oxley soundly, as Morley suspected he knew he would. Then Lords Harrington and Parmenter threw their cards down. That left Morley's cards. Morley had won. Gerald knew he'd won. He eyed him above his cards. "What is this about?"

"Lay out your cards, man. On with it." Gerald's smile couldn't grow any larger, and even though Morley had just grown significantly more wealthy, he didn't trust his oldest friend.

Morley fanned out his cards and narrowed his eyes. "What are you doing?"

Gerald tipped his glass back and drained its contents. "Losing to my best friend. Come now. It's time for us to return home. Her Grace wants me home early."

"How is she feeling?"

Gerald's face clouded, and Morley regretted the question. Since the man had lost his first wife during childbirth, the prospect of doing it all over again loomed in his mind at all hours. Morley talked to him of it often enough. "She seems in the very prime of health. No one has looked healthier."

"No need to speak optimism in my ear. I know she is well, but then, so was Camilla. All we can do is wait and see. Amelia so wanted a child, and I love my wife too much to leave her alone. So there we have it."

Morley clapped him on the back as they stepped out of White's. "Do you ever consider it odd that when youth, we used each other's titles in preparation for the moment the great weight would fall on our shoulders? And now. You still call me Morley, but I ... don't call you anything but Gerald." He laughed trying to lighten the mood.

"You will always be Morley. Even your mother calls you Morley." He laughed. "Why is that?"

"I couldn't guess. Maybe she loves the title?" He shrugged. "Now, enough mystery. Tell me, what did I just win? What's this all about? These holdings in the south?"

"Remember our visit to Sussex?"

Morley half nodded, and then he stopped dead in the street. "When we went to save you from Lady Rochester? And we paid a visit to a family of ladies?" His eyes narrowed. Unbidden, Miss Standish's face came into his mind. "What did you do?"

"I inherited their castle, if you recall."

"I recall a heap of rubble with a few standing rooms."

"Well, we've been fixing it up, and the ladies are just about ready to move in. Five women, all of age. June, the eldest, is not quite twenty three, the youngest sixteen. You won the whole lot of them, with some other holdings besides. The winnings should cover the remaining repairs and upkeep for a time as well."

"I won't take it."

"You have no choice. There were witnesses."

Morley was silent for so long he hoped Gerald began to half suspect he'd truly overstepped his generosity at long last. Then he shook his head. "I know what you're doing, and she doesn't want anything to do with me."

"I don't know what you're talking about."

"And she will want even *less* to do with me if she thinks she is in any way beholden to me, so whatever plans you have going, you can just take back your properties and your pesky family of women and leave me in peace."

"Morley, you're my oldest and best friend. Would I really foist these women on you if I didn't think it would make you the happiest of men? They're from the Northumberland line. Excellent family heritage. The Queen herself takes an interest in their well-being."

"I care not for any of such nonsense, and you know it. You are not to be a matchmaker. It doesn't suit you. And you're terrible at it."

"How would you know, since I've never attempted such a roll until now?"

"So you admit it?"

"I admit nothing. Now, come, don't be cross. You'll upset Amelia."

"Oh, that is low, bringing your wife's condition into this."

They stepped into the townhome, where Simmons took their hats and gloves and overcoats. Gerald waved Morley in. "Thank you for staying with us while you're in town."

"At times, I prefer your home to my own situation."

"You're a good son, though."

Morley hoped he was, though his mother was tiring at best and liked to have her fingers in most aspects of his dealings. He loved her, and felt she was happy in her life, such as it was.

A soft, melodic voice called, "Gerald? Is that you?"

Amelia stepped out into the foyer. "And Morley." She clapped her hands, and the smile that lit her face filled the room.

He accepted her kiss on the cheek and watched as Gerald turned all of his focus to his wife.

Morley bowed. "I will bid you good night. Tomorrow, Gerald, we will discuss your sneaking ways."

"What has he done?" Amelia could only look with love at the Duke, and Morley felt, for a moment, a pang of loneliness.

"I've done nothing. Morley is just a sore winner."

Morley refused to say more. He bowed to Amelia and made his way up the stairs. Before he reached the first landing, he turned. "Oh, and Gerald?"

Gerald turned from his wife for a brief moment.

"When are we to go visit my winnings?"

"Oh, you're on your own with that one, Morley. They will much prefer you to me at any rate." He turned back to Her Grace, and Morley continued up the stairs, his mood darkening with every step.

Gerald had gone too far—in some mad effort to match him with a woman who really had no more interest in Morley than she did dancing a quadrille. June Standish was as practical as he'd seen a person.

He sighed.

And far handsomer than any he'd yet laid eyes on. Her hair was gold—it looked to be spun from the metal itself—and her eyes large, doe-like. He had lost all sense of conversation when he first saw her. It had taken many minutes for him to gain his faculties enough to speak coherently, but she had seemed entirely unaffected. And so that was it for them.

He could only imagine her reaction when he returned to let her know a new gentleman, he himself, was now lord over her life and well-being. Gerald should not toy with others' lives. He needed to be stopped. But Morley wasn't going to be the one to stop him. They'd carried on in their friendship in just this way since they'd known each other. Perhaps he could appeal to Amelia. She had more control over the man than anyone.

What did he need with a decrepit, dilapidated castle? It was an old seat of the royal dukes, so there was a certain level of prestige associated with the place—and with the women. They were of the ancient Normandy family lines. Someone somewhere in their family had wasted their money and left nothing for the line to live off of, but it was still considered an elevated situation if you were on friendly terms with any of the Sisters of Sussex, as they were called.

Sleep did not come easily, and morning was not friendly to Morley's tired eyes and mind. Instead of breaking his fast with Gerald and Amelia, he left for a walk. Oddly, his steps took him to Amelia's old tearoom. They let it out, once she was to become the duchess, and someone else ran the establishment instead. As he stood in the doorway, he almost walked away without entering. What was he doing in a tearoom? Colorful dresses filled the shop to bursting.

"Lord Morley!" With the swish of skirts, a woman's hands were on his arm. "What a pleasant surprise. You must join us for tea. We are discussing the upcoming McAllister ball."

He allowed himself to be led to their table, and when four expectant female eyes turned their hopeful expression toward him, he could only smile and say, "How perfect, for I was just wondering about the details."

"Then you are attending?" Lady Annabelle's eyes lit with such a calculating energy, he shifted in his seat, eyeing the door for a second.

"I am, indeed."

"How provident. Then we shall all be there together. You remember we all became acquainted at the opera one week past. Miss Talbot, Miss Melanie—"

"And Lady Annabelle. Naturally, we are acquainted. It is a pleasure to see you again. I hope your mother is well?"

Lady Annabelle poured his tea, and his mind could not leave the family he'd just won charge of. What sort of women was this new family of sisters? He'd been most impressed with them when considering them as Gerald's wards, of a sort. But now that he owned the house they lived in, he felt a whole new interest in their deportment. Could they pour a man's tea? Stand up well with the other ladies at a ball? Would he be able to marry them off? That was the crux of it. And dash it all, why must he be concerned with the marrying off of anyone? He was in over his head. He needed help. He could appeal to Amelia's sense of grace, but she would have little knowledge of the ways of the *ton*.

The women chattered around him, and he almost sloshed his tea in the saucer when he heard mention of the very women who so aggravated his thoughts.

"They call them the Sisters of Sussex."

"Really? Who are they?"

"The Duke of Northumberland's relations, from a royal line. They are the talk of the *ton* and favorites of many of the noble families. We ourselves have stopped by with some of last season's gowns."

"Five sisters, you say? And they live in the old castle?"

"A cottage nearby. The castle is being renovated, though. I heard the Duke of Granbury has become involved." Lady Annabelle turned to him. "Do you know much about the sisters?"

He cleared his throat and shifted in his seat. "I have met them."

The other ladies leaned forward, eyes on him.

"And I found them charming," he said. "I think you know more about their history than I. Though I do know the castle will be repaired and livable, as it deserves to be. It's a remarkable structure."

Miss Talbot fanned her face. "I should like to visit. I love old buildings and their architecture."

"Do you?" Morley tipped his head to her. She was a pretty sort of woman. Chestnut curls lined her face, and deep brown eyes smiled at him.

"Yes, I like to draw them, and then study them after."

"Interesting. Perhaps we shall meet up there sometime."

"Oh?" Lady Annabelle rested a hand on his arm. "Will you be spending much time in Brighton?"

He hadn't planned on it yet. He'd hoped to stay as far away as possible until his mind wrapped around this new responsibility. But he changed his plans in the moment. "I think I shall." He looked into each of their faces. They were pleasant women. They seemed kind—unassuming, perhaps. "Might I ask for some assistance?"

"Certainly." Lady Annabelle's eyes gleamed.

"I wonder, if I were to assist the ladies—any ladies— to be prepared for a smallish Season in Brighton, do they have a dressmaker or shops enough down there?"

"Oh, certainly. Not nearly as grand or varied as London, but a woman can make do with what Brighton has to offer. The Brighton Royal Pavilion has brought much of the *ton* and a higher level of prestige to the area."

"Thank you."

Their gossip-loving ears seemed to perk right up and all three pairs of eyes looked on him a bit too keenly. He resisted adjusting his cravat. "So, who will be attending the McAllister ball? And have each of you found partners already for your dances?"

The chatter grew more excited, and they listed all the people who were coming or might be coming, depending on the attendance of others. He lingered as long as was polite, and then excused himself from this cheery group.

He would go check in on his mother, though he planned not to mention his new winnings at the table, and then make arrangements to travel down to visit the Standish sisters. God willing, he could establish good solutions for their situation and living and have them well in hand within a few weeks.

To be continued in Book Two in the series: The Earl's Winning Wager. The Earl's Winning Wager

FOLLOW JEN

The next book in the Lords for the Sisters of Sussex.
The Earl's Winning Wager

Jen's other published books

The Nobleman's Daughter
Two lovers in disguise

Scarlet
The Pimpernel retold

A Lady's Maid
Can she love again?

Spun of Gold
Rumplestilskin Retold

Dating the Duke
Time Travel: Regency man in NYC

Charmed by His Lordship
The antics of a fake friendship

Tabitha's Folly
Four over protective Brothers

To read Damen's Secret
The Villain's Romance

Follow her Newsletter

AUTHOR NOTES

A note about mourning in the Regency time period. Women and men practiced a custom of mourning for a full year when a member of their family passed on. They would alter their clothing, wear bands on their arms and avoid social functions where merriment was involved. Women would not participate in courtships. However, men with young children were often encouraged to seek a courtship and another partner to help fill a void for the children even before their time of mourning had passed.

There was a duke who was associated with a castle who had a terrible time of things. His wife died in child birth. His second wife was shortly after committed to bedlam. He tried several affairs. His tragic story intrigued me. My duke has a different story and result of his life choices, but The Duke of Granbury's experiences are motivated in part by the real life happenings of another.

Made in the USA
Monee, IL
21 August 2022